KU-076-876

CONTENTS

CHAPTER ONE

George is all alone

'I DO think it's *mean*,' said George, fiercely. 'Why can't I go when the others do? I've had two weeks at home, and haven't seen the others since school broke up. And now they're off for a wonderful fortnight and I'm not with them.'

'Don't be silly, George,' said her mother. 'You can go as soon as that cold of yours is better.'

'It's better now,' said George, scowling. 'Mother, you know it is!'

'That's enough, Georgina,' said her father, looking up from his newspaper. 'This is the third breakfast-time we've had this argument. Be quiet.'

George would never answer anyone when she was called Georgina – so, much as she would have liked to say something back, she pursed up her mouth and looked away.

Her mother laughed. 'Oh, George, dear! Don't look so terribly fierce. It was your own fault you got this cold – you *would* go and bathe and stay in far too long and after all, it's only the third week in April!'

'I always bathe in April,' said George, sulkily.

'I said "BE QUIET",' said her father, banging down his paper on the table. 'One more word from you, George, and you won't go to your three cousins at all.'

'Woof,' said Timmy, from under the table. He didn't like it when anyone spoke angrily to George.

'And don't *you* start arguing with me, either,' said George's father, poking Timmy with his toe, and scowling exactly like George.

His wife laughed again. 'Oh, be quiet, the two of you,' she said. 'George, be patient dear. I'll let you go off to your cousins as soon as ever I can – tomorrow, if you're good, and don't cough much today.'

'Oh, Mother – why didn't you say so before?' said George, her scowl disappearing like magic. 'I didn't cough once in the night. I'm perfectly all right today. Oh, if I can go off to Faynights Castle tomorrow, I *promise* I won't cough once today!'

'What's this about Faynights Castle?' demanded her father, looking up again. 'First I've heard of it!'

'Oh no, Quentin dear, I've told you at least three times,' said his wife. 'Julian, Dick and Anne have been lent two funny old caravans by a school friend. They are in a field near Faynights Castle.'

2

'Oh. So they're not *staying* in a castle, then,' said George's father. 'Can't have that. I won't have George coming home all high and mighty.'

'George couldn't *possibly* be high and mighty,' said his wife. 'It's as much as I can do to get her to keep her nails clean and wear clean jeans. Do be sensible, Quentin. You know perfectly well that George and her cousins always like to go off on extraordinary holidays together.'

'And have adventures,' grinned George, who was in a very good temper indeed at the thought of going to join her cousins the next day.

'No. You're not to have any of those awful adventures this time,' said her mother. 'Anyway, I don't see how you can, staying in a peaceful place like the village of Faynights Castle, living in a couple of old caravans.'

'I wouldn't trust George anywhere,' said her husband. 'Give her just a *sniff* of an adventure, and she's after it. I never knew anyone like George. Thank goodness we've only got one child. I don't feel as if I could cope with two or three Georges.'

'There are plenty of people like George,' said his wife. 'Julian and Dick for instance. Always in the middle of something or other – with Anne tagging behind, longing for a peaceful life.'

'Well, I've had enough of this argument,' said

3

George's father, pushing his chair out vigorously, and accidentally kicking Timmy under the table. He yelped.

'That dog's got no brains,' said the impatient man. 'Lies under the table at every meal and expects me to remember he's there! Well, I'm going to do some work.'

He went out of the room. The dining-room door banged. Then the study door banged. Then a window was shut with a bang. A fire was poked very vigorously. There was the creak of an armchair as someone sat down in it heavily. Then there was silence.

'Now your father's lost to the world till lunchtime,' said George's mother. 'Dear, oh dear – I've told him at *least* three times about Faynights Castle, where your cousins are staying, bless him. Now, George, I do really think you can go tomorrow, dear – you look so much better today. You can get your things ready and I'll pack them this afternoon.'

'Thank you, Mother,' said George, giving her a sudden hug. 'Anyway, Father will be glad to have me out of the house for a bit! I'm too noisy for him!'

'You're a pair!' said her mother, remembering the slammed doors and other things. 'You're both a perfect nuisance at times, but I couldn't bear to do without you! Oh, Timmy, are you still under the table? I wish you wouldn't leave your tail about so! Did I hurt you?'

'Oh, he doesn't mind *you* treading on it, Mother,' said George, generously. 'I'm going to get my things ready this very minute. How do I get to Faynights Castle? By train?'

'Yes. I'll take you to Kirrin Station, and you can catch the ten-forty,' said her mother. 'You change at Limming Ho, and take the train that goes to Faynights. If you send a card to Julian, he'll get it tomorrow morning and will meet you.'

'I'll write it now,' said George, happily. 'Oh, Mother, I began to be afraid this awful cold would hang on all through the holidays! I shan't bathe again on such a cold day in April.'

'You said that last year – and the year before that too,' said her mother. 'You have a very short memory, George!'

'Come on, Timmy!' said George, and the two of them went out of the door like a whirlwind. It slammed behind them, and the house shook.

At once the study door opened and an angry voice yelled loudly: 'Who's that slamming doors when I'm at work? Can't ANYBODY in this house shut a door quietly?'

George grinned as she fled upstairs. The biggest slammer-of-doors was her father, but he only heard the slams made by other people. George turned her writing-case inside out to find a postcard. She must post it at once or Julian wouldn't get it – and it *would* be so nice to have all her three cousins meeting her!

'We're off tomorrow,' she told Timmy, who looked up at her and wagged his tail vigorously. 'Yes, you're coming too, of course – then the Five will all be together again. The Famous Five! You'll like that, won't you, Tim? So shall I!'

She scribbled the postcard and flew down to post it. Slam went the front door, and her father almost jumped out of his skin. He was a very clever and hardworking scientist, impatient, hot-tempered, kindly and very forgetful. How he wished his daughter was not so exactly like him, but was like his quiet, gentle little niece Anne!

George posted the card. It was short and to the point.

Cold gone. Coming tomorrow. Arriving 12.05 so make sure you all meet me and Timmy. Our tails are well up, I can tell you!

GEORGE.

George turned out her drawers and began to pick out the things she wanted to take with her. Her mother came to help. There was always an argument about packing, because George wanted to take as little as possible, and no warm things at all, and her mother had exactly opposite ideas.

However, between the two of them they managed to pack the suitcase full of quite sensible things. George refused as usual to take a dress of any sort.

'I wonder when you'll grow out of wanting to be a boy, and of acting like one!' said her mother, exasperated. 'All right, all right – take those awful old jeans if you want to, and that red jersey. But you *are* to pack those warm vests. I put them in once, and you took them out. And you must take a warm rug, Julian says. The caravans are not very warm in this weather.'

'I wonder what they're like,' said George, stuffing the vests in. 'They're funny, old-fashioned ones, Julian said in his letter. Perhaps they're like the ones the travellers have – not the modern, streamlined ones that are pulled along by cars.'

'You'll see tomorrow,' said her mother. 'Oh, George – you're coughing again!'

'Just the dust, that's all,' said George going purple in the face trying to hold back the tickle in her throat. She drank a glass of water in a hurry. It would be too dreadful if her mother said she wasn't to go after all!

However, her mother really did think that George was better. She had been in bed for a week, making a terrible fuss, and being a very difficult patient. Now, after being up for a few days she really seemed herself again.

'It will do her good to get down to Faynights and its good, strong air,' thought her mother. 'She needs company again, too – she doesn't like having to be all alone, knowing the others are holidaying without her.'

George felt happy that evening. Only one more night and she would be off to a fortnight's caravanning! If only the weather was good, what a fine time they would have!

Suddenly the telephone shrilled out. R-r-r-r-r-ring! R-r-r-r-ring!

George's mother went to answer it. 'Hallo!' she said. 'Oh – it's you, Julian. Is everything all right?'

George sped out into the hall at once. Oh, surely, surely, nothing had happened! Surely Julian wasn't ringing to tell her not to come! She listened breathlessly.

'What's that you say, Julian? I can't make out what you're talking about, dear. Yes, of course, your uncle is all right. Why shouldn't he be? No, he hasn't disappeared. Julian, what *are* you talking about?'

George listened impatiently. What *was* all this? But it

turned out to be something quite ordinary, really. When at last her mother put down the receiver, she told George.

'Don't hop about like that, George. It's *quite* all right, you can go tomorrow. Julian was only ringing up to make sure that your father wasn't one of the scientists who have suddenly disappeared. Apparently in tonight's paper there is a short report about two that have completely vanished – and dear old Julian wanted to make sure your father was here safely!'

'As if Father would vanish!' said George, scornfully. 'Julian must be mad! It's just two more of those silly scientists who are disloyal to this country, and disappear to another country to sell our secrets! *I* could have told Julian that!'

CHAPTER TWO

All together again

NEXT MORNING, on a dewy hillside a good distance from Kirrin, where George lived, two boys leapt down the steps of a caravan, and went to one nearby. They rapped on the door.

'Anne! Are you awake? It's a heavenly day!'

'Of course I'm awake!' cried a voice. 'The door's unlocked. Come in. I'm getting breakfast.'

Julian and Dick pushed open the blue-painted door. Anne was standing at a little stove at one end of her caravan, boiling eggs in a saucepan.

'I can't look round,' she said. 'I'm timing them by my watch. One minute more to go.'

'The postman has just brought a card from George,' said Julian. 'She says her tail and Timmy's are both well up! I'm glad she's coming at last – and old Timmy too.'

'We'll all go and meet her,' said Anne, still with her eyes on her watch. 'Twenty seconds more.'

'We only came here ourselves three days ago,' said Dick. 'So she hasn't really missed much. Surely those eggs will be hard-boiled, Anne!'

Anne stopped looking at her watch. 'No, they won't. They'll be just right.' She scooped them out of the little saucepan with a big spoon. 'Put them in the egg-cups, Dick. There they are – just under your nose.'

Dick picked an egg up from the plate on which Anne had placed them. It was so hot that he dropped it with a yell, and it broke its shell. Yolk flowed out of it.

'DICK! You *saw* me take it out of boiling water!' said Anne. 'Now I've got to do another. It's a pity old Timmy isn't here. He'd soon have licked that broken egg up from the floor and saved me clearing up the mess.'

'We'll eat our breakfast sitting on the steps of your caravan, Anne,' said Julian. 'The sun's so lovely.'

So they all sat there, eating boiled eggs, well-buttered bread with chunky, home-made marmalade afterwards, and then juicy apples. The sun shone down and Julian took off his coat.

Their two caravans were set on a sloping, grassy hillside. A tall hedge grew behind, and kept off the wind. Primroses ran in a pale gold streak under the hedge, and brilliant celandines shone in the sun, turning their polished faces towards it.

Not far off were three more caravans, but they were modern ones. The people staying in those were not yet up, and the doors were fast shut. The three children had had no chance of making friends with them.

On the opposite hill rose an old, ruined castle, whose great walls still defied the gales that sometimes blew over the hills. It had four towers. Three were very much broken, but the fourth looked almost complete. The windows were slit-holes, made centuries back when archers shot their arrows from them.

A very steep pathway led up to the castle. At the top of it was a gateway, enormously strong, built of big white blocks of stone. The gateway was now filled by a great screen of wrought iron to prevent anyone entering, and the only entrance was by a small tower in which was a narrow door. Here there was a turnstile through which visitors might go to see the old castle.

A high, strong wall ran all round the castle, still standing after so many years. Bits of the top of it had fallen down the hill and lay half-buried in grass and weeds. It had once been a magnificent old castle, built on the high, steep hill for safety, a place from which the castle guards might see the country easily for miles around.

As Julian said, anyone up in one of the towers, or even on the wall, would be able to see enemies approaching from seven counties. There would be plenty of time to shut the great gate, man the walls, and get ready to withstand quite a long siege if necessary.

The three of them sat on the steps, lazing in the sun, when they had finished their breakfast. They looked at the ruined old castle, and watched the jackdaws circling round the four towers.

'There must be about a thousand jackdaws there,' said Dick. 'I wish we had field-glasses so that we could watch them. It would be as good as a circus. I love the way they all fly up together, and circle round and round and yet never bump into one another.'

'Do they nest in that old castle?' asked Anne.

'Oh, yes – they fill up the towers with big sticks,' said Dick, 'and put their nests on the top. I bet we'd find the ground beneath the towers strewn ankle-deep in sticks if we went to see.'

'Well, let's go one day when George is here,' said Anne. 'It only costs five pence to go in. I like old castles. I like the *feel* of old places.'

'So do I,' said Julian. 'I hope George brings the field-glasses she had for her birthday. We could take them up into the castle with us and see all round the countryside for miles and miles. We could count the seven counties!'

'I must wash up,' said Anne, getting up. 'I must tidy

the caravans too before George comes.'

'You don't really think old George will notice if they're tidy or not, do you?' said Dick. 'It will be a waste of your time, Anne!'

But Anne always enjoyed tidying things and putting them away in cupboards or on shelves. She liked having the two caravans to look after. She had just got used to them nicely and was looking forward to showing George round them.

She skipped over to the hedge and picked a great bunch of primroses. Back she went and divided them into two. She stuffed half into one little blue bowl, set their green crinkled leaves round them, and then put the other half into a second bowl.

'There – you go with the green and yellow curtains!' she said. She was soon very busy sweeping and dusting. She debated whether to send Dick to the stream to wash the breakfast things, and decided not to. Dick wasn't too good with crockery, and it was not theirs to break – it belonged to the owner of the caravans.

By the time it was half past eleven the caravans were spick and span. George's sheets and blankets were on the shelf above her bunk, which, in the daytime, let down neatly against the wall to make more room. Anne had a bunk on the opposite side.

'This is the kind of holiday I *like*,' said Anne to herself. 'Somewhere small to live, fields and hills just outside, picnicky meals – and not too much adventure!'

'What are you murmuring about, Anne?' said Dick peeping in at the window. 'Did I hear something about adventure? Are you looking for one already?'

'Good gracious no!' said Anne. 'It's the last thing I want! And the last thing we'll get too, in this quiet little place, thank goodness.'

Dick grinned. 'Well, you never know,' he said. 'Are you ready to come and meet George, Anne? It's about time we went.'

Anne went down the steps and joined Dick and Julian. 'Better lock the door,' said Dick. 'We've locked ours.' He locked Anne's door and the three set off down the grassy hillside to the stile that led into the lane below. The old castle on the opposite hill seemed to tower up higher and higher as they went down towards the village.

'It will be lovely to see Timmy again,' said Anne. 'And I'll be jolly glad to have George too, in my caravan. I didn't really *mind* being alone at night – but it's always nice to have George near me, and Timmy grunting in his sleep.'

'You want to share a room with Dick if you like

grunts and snorts and moans,' said Julian. 'What *do* you dream about, Dick? You must have more nightmares than anyone else in the kingdom!'

'I *never* grunt or snort or moan,' said Dick indignantly. 'You want to hear yourself! Why . . .'

'Look – isn't that the train coming in – isn't that it curving round the line in the distance?' said Anne. 'It must be! There's only one train in the morning here! We'd better run!'

They ran at top speed. The train drew in at the station just as they raced on to the platform. A head of short, curly hair looked out from a window – and then another brown head just below it.

'George – and Timmy!' yelled Anne.

'Hallo!' shouted George, almost falling out of the door.

'WOOF!' barked Timmy, and leapt down to the platform almost on top of Dick. Down jumped George, her eyes shining. She hugged Anne, and gave Julian and Dick a playful shove each. 'I'm here!' she said. 'I felt awful knowing you were away camping without me. I gave poor old Mother a dreadful time.'

'I bet you did,' said Julian, and linked his arm in hers. 'Let me take that suitcase. We'll just slip into the village first and have a few ice-creams to celebrate.

There's a shop here that has some jolly decent ones.'

'Good. I feel exactly like ice-creams,' said George, happily. 'Look, Timmy knows what you said. His tongue is hanging out for an ice-cream already. Timmy, aren't you pleased we're all together again?'

'Woof,' said Timmy, and licked Anne's hand for the twentieth time.

'I really ought to bring a towel with me when I meet Timmy,' said Anne. 'His licks are so very wet. Oh no, not *again*, Timmy – go and use your tongue on Julian!'

'I say, look – George *has* brought her field-glasses with her!' said Dick, suddenly noticing that the brown strap over George's shoulder did not belong to a camera but to a very fine leather case that held the new field-glasses. 'Good! We wanted to watch the jackdaws with them – and there are some herons down on the marsh too.'

'Well, I thought I *must* bring them,' said George. 'It's the first hols I've had a chance to use them. Mother wouldn't let me take them to school. I say – how much further is this ice-cream shop?'

'In the dairy here,' said Julian, marching her in. 'And I advise you to start off with vanilla, go on to strawberry and finish up with chocolate.'

'You do have good ideas!' said George. 'I hope you've

got some money as well, if we're going to eat ice-creams at this rate. Mother didn't give me very much to spend.'

They sat down and ordered ice-creams. The plump little shop-woman smiled at them. She knew them by now. 'This is very good weather for you,' she said. 'Are there many caravanners up on Faynights Field?'

'No, not many,' said Julian, beginning his ice.

'Well, you're going to have a few more,' said the little plump lady. 'I hear there's some fair-folk coming – they usually camp up in your field. You'll have some fun if so.'

'Oh, good!' said Dick. 'We'll really be able to make a few friends then. We like fair-folk, don't we, Timmy?'

CHAPTER THREE

A pleasant morning

'IS THERE going to be a fair near here then?' asked George, starting on her strawberry ice. 'What sort of a fair? A circus or something?'

'No. Just a mixed-up show,' said the shop-woman. 'There's to be a fire-eater, and that'll bring the villagers to the show faster than anything. A fire-eater! Did you ever hear of such a thing? I wonder that anyone cares to make a living at that!'

'What else is there to be?' asked Anne. She didn't somehow fancy watching anyone eating fire!

'Well, there's a man who can get himself free in under two minutes, no matter how tightly he's tied up with rope,' said the woman. 'Fair miracle he must be! And there's a man called Mr India-rubber, because he can bend himself anywhere, and wriggle through drain-pipes and get in at a window if it's left open just a crack!'

'Gracious! He'd make a good burglar!' said George. 'I wish I was like india-rubber! Can this man bounce when he falls down?'

Everyone laughed. 'What else?' said Anne. 'This sounds very exciting.'

'There's a man with snakes,' said the plump little lady with a shudder. 'Snakes! Just fancy! I'd be afraid they would bite me. I'd run a mile if I saw a snake coming at me.'

'Are they poisonous snakes that he has, I wonder?' said Dick. 'I don't somehow fancy having a caravan next to ours with lashings of poisonous snakes crawling round.'

'Don't!' said Anne. 'I should go home at once.'

Another customer came in and the shop-woman had to leave the children and go to serve her. The four felt rather thrilled. What a bit of luck to have such exciting people in the same field as they were!

'A fire-eater!' said Dick. 'I've always wanted to see one. I bet he doesn't *really* eat fire! He'd burn the whole of his mouth and throat.'

'Has everyone finished?' asked Julian, getting some money out of his pocket. 'If so, we'll take George up to the field and show her our painted caravans. They aren't a bit like the ones we once went caravanning in, George – they are old-fashioned travellers' ones. You'll like them. Colourful and very picturesque.'

'Who lent you them?' asked George, as they left

the shop. 'Some school friend, wasn't it?'

'Yes. He and his family always go and camp in their caravans in the Easter and summer hols,' said Julian. 'But this Easter they're going to France – and rather than leave them empty, they thought they'd lend them out – and we're the lucky ones!'

They walked up the lane and came to the stile. George looked up at the towering castle, gleaming in the sun on the hill opposite.

'Faynights Castle,' she said. 'Hundreds of years old! How I'd love to know all the things that happened there through the centuries. I do love old things. I vote we go and explore it.'

'We will. It only costs five pence,' said Dick. 'We'll all have a good five pence worth of castle. I wonder if there are any dungeons. Dark, damp, drear and dreadful!'

They went up the grassy hillside to the field where their caravans were. George exclaimed in delight. 'Oh! Are *those* our caravans? Aren't they lovely? They're just like the caravans the travellers use – only these look cleaner and brighter.'

'The red caravan, picked out with black and yellow, is ours,' said Dick. 'The blue one, picked out in black and yellow, is yours and Anne's.'

'Woof,' said Timmy at once.

'Oh, sorry – yours *too*, Timmy,' said Dick at once, and everyone chuckled. It was funny the way Timmy suddenly made a woofish remark, just as if he really understood every word that was said. George was quite certain he did, of course.

The caravans stood on high wheels. There was a window on each side. The door was at the front, and so were the steps, of course. Bright curtains hung at the windows, and a line of bold carving ran round the edges of the out-jutting roof.

'They are old traveller caravans painted and made really up to date,' said Julian. 'They're jolly comfortable inside too – bunks that fold down against the walls in the daytime – a little sink for washing-up, though we usually use the stream, because it's such a bore to fetch water – a small larder, cupboards and shelves – cork carpet on the floor with warm rugs so that no draught comes through . . .'

'You sound as if you are trying to sell them to me!' said George, with a laugh. 'You needn't! I love them both, and I think they're miles nicer than the modern caravans down there. Somehow these seem *real*!'

'Oh, the others are real enough,' said Julian. 'And they've got more space – but space doesn't matter to us because we shall live outside most of the time.'

'Do we have a camp-fire?' asked George, eagerly. 'Oh, yes – I see we do. There's the ashy patch where you had your fire. Oh, Julian, do let's have a fire there at night and sit round it in the darkness!'

'With midges biting us and bats flapping all round,' said Dick. 'Yes, certainly we will! Come inside, George.'

'She's to come into my caravan first,' said Anne, and pushed George up the steps. George was really delighted.

She was very happy to think she was going to have a peaceful two weeks here with her three cousins and Timmy. She pulled her bunk up and down to see how it worked. She opened the larder and cupboard doors. Then she went to see the boys' caravan.

'How *tidy*!' she said, in surprise. 'I expected Anne's to be tidy – but yours is just as spick and span. Oh dear – I hope you haven't all turned over a new leaf and become models of neatness – *I* haven't!'

'Don't worry,' said Dick, with a grin. 'Anne has been at work – you know how she loves to put everything in its place. We don't need to worry about anything when she's about. Good old Anne!'

'All the same, George will have to help,' said Anne,

firmly. 'We've all got to tidy up and cook and do things like that.'

George groaned. 'All right, Anne, I'll do my share – sometimes. I say – there won't be much room for Timmy on my bunk at nights, will there?'

'Well, he's not coming on mine,' said Anne. 'He can sleep on the floor on a rug. Can't you, Timmy?'

'Woof,' said Timmy, without wagging his tail at all. He looked very disapproving.

'There you are – he says he wouldn't *dream* of doing such a thing!' said George. 'He *always* sleeps on my feet.'

They went outside again. It really was a lovely day. The primroses opened more and more of their little yellow flowers, and a blackbird suddenly burst into a fluting song on the bough of a hawthorn tree in the hedge nearby.

'Did anyone get a paper in the village?' asked Dick. 'Oh, you did, Julian. Good. Let's have a look at the weather forecast. If it's good we might go for a long walk this afternoon. The sea is not really very far off.'

Julian took the folded paper from his pocket and threw it over to Dick. He sat down on the steps of the caravan and opened it.

He was looking for the paragraph giving the weather

forecast when headlines caught his eye. He gave an exclamation.

'Hallo! Here's a bit more about those two vanished scientists, Julian!'

'Oh!' said George, remembering Julian's telephone call of the night before. 'Julian, whatever in the world made you think my father could be one of the vanished scientists? As if he would ever be disloyal to his country and take his secrets anywhere else!'

'Oh, I didn't think that,' said Julian, at once. 'Of *course* I didn't! I'd never think Uncle Quentin would do a thing like that. No – in yesterday's paper it just said that two of our most famous scientists had disappeared – and I thought perhaps they had been kidnapped. And as Uncle Quentin is really very famous, I just thought I'd ring up to make sure.'

'Oh,' said George. 'Well, as Mother hadn't heard a thing about them she was awfully astonished when you asked her if Father had disappeared. Especially as he was banging about just then in the study, looking for something he had lost.'

'Which he was sitting on as usual, I suppose,' said Dick with a grin. 'But listen to this – it doesn't look as if the two men have been kidnapped – it looks as if they just walked out and took important papers with them!

Beasts! There's too much of that sort of thing nowadays, it seems to me!'

He read out a paragraph or two.

'Derek Terry-Kane and Jeffrey Pottersham have been missing for two days. They met at a friend's house to discuss a certain aspect of their work, and then left together to walk to the Underground. Since then they have not been seen.

'It has, however, been established that Terry-Kane had brought his passport up to date and had purchased tickets for flying to Paris. No news of his arrival there has been reported.'

'There! Just what I said to Mother!' exclaimed George. 'They've gone off to sell their secrets to another country. Why do we let them?'

'Uncle Quentin won't be pleased about that,' said Julian. 'Didn't he work with Terry-Kane at one time?'

'Yes, I believe he did,' said George. 'I'm jolly glad I'm not at home today – Father will be rampaging round like anything, telling Mother hundreds of times what he thinks about scientists who are traitors!'

'He certainly will,' said Julian. 'I don't blame him either. That's a thing I don't understand – to be a traitor to one's own country. It leaves a nasty taste in my mouth to think of it. Come on – let's think about dinner, Anne. What are we going to have?'

'Fried sausages and onions, potatoes, a tin of sliced peaches, and I'll make a custard,' said Anne, at once.

'I'll fry the sausages,' said Dick. 'I'll light the fire out here and get the frying-pan. Anyone like their sausages split in the cooking?'

Everyone did. 'I like mine nice and *burnt*,' said George. 'How many do we have each? I've only had those ice-creams since breakfast.'

'There are twelve,' said Anne, giving Dick the bag. 'Three each. None for Timmy! But I've got a large, juicy bone for him. Julian, will you get me some water, please? There's the pail, over there. I want to peel the potatoes. George, can you possibly open the peaches without cutting yourself like you did last time?'

'Yes, Captain!' said George, with a grin. 'Ah – this is like old times. Good food, good company and a good time. Three cheers for Us!'

CHAPTER FOUR

The fair-folk arrive

THAT FIRST day they were all together was a lovely one.
They enjoyed it thoroughly, especially George, who
had fretted all by herself for two weeks at home. Timmy
was very happy too. He tore after rabbits, most of them
quite imaginary, up and down the field and in and out
the hedges till he was tired out.

Then he would come and fling himself down by the
four, panting like a steam-engine going uphill, his long
pink tongue hanging out of his mouth.

'You make me feel hot just to *look* at you, Timmy,'
sa ' Anne, pushing him away. 'Look, George – he's so
hot 's steaming! One of these days, Timmy, you'll
blow up!'

They went for a walk in the afternoon, but didn't
quite get to the sea. They saw it from a hill, sparkling
blue in the distance. Little white yachts dotted the blue
water like far-off swans with wings outspread. They had
tea at a farmhouse, watched by a couple of big-eyed
farm children.

'Do you want to take some of my home-made jam with you?' asked the farmer's jolly, red-faced wife, when they paid her for their tea.

'Oh, yes, rather!' said Dick. 'And I suppose you couldn't sell us some of that fruit cake? We're camping in caravans in Faynights Field, just opposite the castle – so we're having picnic meals each day.'

'Yes, you can have a whole cake,' said the farmer's wife. 'I did my baking yesterday, so there's plenty. And would you like some ham? And I've some good pickled onions too.'

This was wonderful! They bought all the food very cheaply indeed, and carried it home gladly. Dick took off the lid of the pickled onions halfway back to the caravans, and sniffed.

'Better than any scent!' he said. 'Have a sniff, George.'

It didn't stop at sniffs, of course. Everyone took out a large pickled onion – except Timmy who backed away at once. Onions were one thing he really couldn't bear. Dick put back the lid.

'I think somebody else ought to carry the onions, not Dick,' said Anne. 'There won't be many left by the time we reach our caravans!'

When they climbed over the stile at the bottom of the field the sun was going down. The evening star had appeared in the sky and twinkled brightly. As they trudged up to their caravans Julian stopped and pointed.

'Hallo! Look! There are two more caravans here – rather like ours. I wonder if it's the fair-folk arriving.'

'And there's another one, see – coming up the lane,' said Dick. 'It will have to go to the field-gate because it can't come the way we do – over the stile. There it goes.'

'We shall soon have plenty of exciting neighbours!' said Anne, pleased. They went up to their own caravans and looked curiously at the one that stood near theirs. It was yellow, picked out with blue and black, and could have done with a new coat of paint. It was very like their own caravans, but looked much older.

There didn't seem to be anyone about the newly arrived vans. The doors and windows were shut. The four stood and looked curiously at them.

'There's a big box under the nearest caravan,' said Julian. 'I wonder what's in it!'

The box was long, shallow and wide. On the sides were round holes, punched into it at intervals. George went to the caravan and bent down to look at the box, wondering if there was anything alive in it.

Timmy went with her, sniffing at the holes in curiosity. He suddenly backed away, and barked loudly. George put her hand on his collar to drag him off but he wouldn't go with her. He barked without stopping!

A noise came from inside the box – a rustling, dry, sliding sort of noise that made Timmy bark even more frantically.

'Stop it, Timmy! Stop it!' said George, tugging at him. 'Julian, come and help me. There's something in that box that Timmy has never met before – goodness knows what – and he's half-puzzled and half-scared. He's barking defiance – and he'll never stop unless we drag him away!'

An angry voice came from the bottom of the field by the stile. 'Hey you! Take that dog away! What do you mean by poking into my business – upsetting my snakes!'

'Oooh – snakes!' said Anne, retiring quickly to her own caravan. 'George, it's snakes in there. Do get Timmy away.'

Julian and George managed to drag Timmy away, half-choking him with his collar, though he didn't seem to notice this at all. The angry voice was now just behind them. George turned and saw a little man, middle-aged, with gleaming black eyes. He was shaking his fist, still shouting.

'Sorry,' said George, pulling Timmy harder. 'Please stop shouting, or my dog will go for you.'

'Go for me! He will go for me! You keep a dangerous dog like that, which smells out my snakes and will go for me!' yelled the angry little man, dancing about like a boxer on his toes. 'Ahhhhhh! Wait till I let out my snakes – and then your dog will run and run, and will never be seen again!'

This was a most alarming threat. With an enormous heave, Julian, Dick and George at last got Timmy under control, dragged him up the steps of Anne's caravan, and shut the door on him. Anne tried to quieten him, while the other three went out to the angry little man again.

He had dragged out the big, shallow box, and had opened the lid. The three watched, fascinated. What snakes had he in there? Rattlesnakes? Cobras? They were all ready to run for their lives if the snakes were as angry as their owner.

A great head reared itself out of the box, and swung itself from side to side. Two unblinking dark eyes gleamed – and then a long, long body writhed out and glided up the man's legs, round his waist and round his neck. He fondled it, talking in a low, caressing voice.

George shivered. Julian and Dick watched in amazement. 'It's a python,' said Julian. 'My, what a monster. I've never seen one so close before. I wonder it doesn't wind itself round that fellow and squeeze him to death.'

'He's got hold of it near the tail,' said Dick, watching. 'Oh, look – there's another one!'

Sure enough a second python slid out of the box, coil upon gleaming coil. It too wreathed itself round its owner, making a loud hissing noise as it did so. Its body was thicker than Julian's calf.

Anne was watching out of her caravan window, hardly able to believe her eyes. She had never in her life seen snakes as big as these. She didn't even know what they were. She began to wish their caravans were miles and miles away.

The little man quieted his snakes at last. They almost hid him with their great coils! From each side of his neck came a snake's head, flat and shining.

Timmy was now watching out of the window also, his head beside Anne's. He was amazed to see the gliding snakes, and stopped barking at once. He got down from the window and went under the table. Timmy didn't think he liked the look of these new creatures at all!

The man fondled the snakes and then, still speaking to them lovingly, got them back into their box again. They glided in, and piled themselves inside, coil upon coil. The man shut down the lid and locked it.

Then he turned to the three watching children. 'You see how upset you make my snakes?' he said. 'Now you keep away, you hear? And you keep your dog away too. Ah, you children! Interfering, poking your noses, staring! I do not like children and nor do my snakes. You KEEP AWAY, SEE?'

He shouted the last words so angrily that the three jumped. 'Look here,' said Julian, 'we only came to say we were sorry our dog barked like that. Dogs always bark at strange things they don't know or understand. It's only natural.'

'Dogs, too, I hate,' said the little man, going into his caravan. 'You will keep him away from here, especially when I have my snakes out, or one might give him too loving a squeeze. Ha!'

He disappeared into his van and the door shut firmly.

'Not so good,' said Julian. 'We seem to have made a bad start with the fair-folk – and I had hoped they would be friendly and let us into some of their secrets.'

'I don't like the last thing he said,' said George, worried. 'A "loving squeeze" by one of those pythons would be the end of Timmy. I shall certainly keep him away when I see that funny little man taking out his snakes. He really seemed to *love* them, didn't he?'

'He certainly did,' said Julian. 'Well, I wonder who

lives in the second newly arrived caravan. I feel I hardly dare even to look at it in case it contains gorillas or elephants or hippos, or . . .'

'Don't be an idiot,' said George. 'Come on, it's getting dark. Hallo, here comes the caravan we saw down in the lane just now!'

It came slowly up the grassy hillside, bumping as it went. On the side was painted a name in large, scarlet letters.

'Mister India-rubber.'

'Oh – the rubber-man!' said George. 'Dick – is he the driver, do you think?'

They all stared at the driver. He was long and thin and droopy, and he looked as if he might burst into tears at any moment. His horse looked rather the same.

'Well – he *might* be Mr India-rubber,' said Julian. 'But certainly there doesn't seem to be much *bounce* in him! Look – he's getting down.'

The man got down with a supple, loose grace that didn't seem to fit his droopy body at all. He took the horse out of the shafts and set it loose in the field. It wandered away, pulling here and there at the grass, still looking as sad and droopy as its master.

'Bufflo!' suddenly yelled the man. 'You in?'

The door of the second caravan opened and a young

man looked out – a huge young man with a mop of yellow hair, a bright red shirt and a broad smile.

'Hiya, Rubber!' he called. 'We got here first. Come along in – Skippy's got some food ready.'

Mr India-rubber walked sadly up the steps of Bufflo's caravan. The door shut.

'This is really rather exciting,' said Dick. 'An india-rubber man – Bufflo and Skippy, whoever they may be – and a man with tame snakes next to us. Whatever next!'

Anne called to them. 'Do come in. Timmy's whining like anything.'

They went up the steps of her caravan and found that Anne had got ready a light supper for them – a ham sandwich each, a piece of fruit cake and an orange.

'I'll have a pickled onion with my sandwich, please,' said Dick. 'I'll chop it up and put it in with the ham. What wonderful ideas I do have, to be sure!'

CHAPTER FIVE

Night and morning

AS THEY had their supper they talked about the strange new arrivals. Timmy sat close to George, trying to tell her that he was sorry for causing such a disturbance. She patted him and scolded him at the same time.

'I quite understand that you don't like the snakes, Timmy – but when I tell you to stop barking and come away you MUST do as you're told! Do you understand?'

Timmy's tail dropped and he put his big head on George's knee. He gave a little whine.

'I don't think he'll ever go near that box again, now he's seen the snakes that came out of it,' said Anne. 'You should have seen how scared he was when he looked out of the window with me and saw them. He went and hid under the table.'

'It's a pity we've made a bad start with the fair-folk,' said Julian. 'I don't expect they like children much, because as a rule the kids would make themselves an awful nuisance – peering here and poking there.'

'I think I can hear more caravans arriving,' said

37

George, and Timmy pricked up his ears and growled. 'Be quiet, Timmy. We're not the only ones allowed in this field!'

Dick went to the window and peered out into the twilight. He saw some large, dark shapes in another part of the field, looming out of the darkness. A little camp-fire burned brightly in front of one, showing a small figure bending over it.

'These are jolly good sandwiches, Anne,' said Dick. 'What about another pickled onion, everyone?'

'No, Dick,' said Anne firmly. 'You've eaten your sandwich.'

'Well, I can eat a pickled onion *without* a sandwich, can't I?' said Dick. 'Hand over, Anne.'

Anne wouldn't. 'I've hidden them,' she said. 'You want some for tomorrow, don't you? Don't be greedy, Dick. Have a biscuit if you're still hungry.'

'I meant to ask if we could have a camp-fire outside tonight,' said George, remembering. 'But somehow I feel so sleepy I think I'd nod off if I sat by it!'

'I feel sleepy too,' said Anne. 'Let's clear up, George, and snuggle into our bunks. The boys can go to their caravan and read or play games if they want to.'

Dick yawned. 'Well – I might read for a bit,' he said. 'I hope you've got enough water, Anne, for the various things you use it for — because I do NOT intend to stumble over this dark field to the stream, and fall over snakes and anything else the fair-folk may have strewn carelessly about the grass!'

'You don't think those snakes could get loose, do you?' said Anne, anxiously.

'Of course not!' said Julian. 'Anyway, Timmy will bark the place down if even a hedgehog comes roving by, so you don't need to worry about snakes!'

The boys said good night and went off to their own caravan. The girls saw a light suddenly shine out there, and shadows moved across the curtains drawn over the windows.

'Dick's lit their lamp,' said Anne. Theirs was already lit, and the caravan looked cosy and friendly. Anne showed George how to put up her bunk. It clicked into place, felt nice and firm and was most inviting-looking.

The girls made their beds in the bunks, putting in sheets and blankets and rugs. 'Where's my pillow?' asked George. 'Oh — it's a cushion in the daytime, is it? What a good idea!'

She and Anne took the covers off the two cushions in the chairs, and underneath were the pillowcases over the pillows, ready for the night!

They undressed, washed in stream water in the little

sink, cleaned their teeth and brushed their hair. 'Does the water go under the caravan when I pull the plug out of the sink?' said George. 'Here goes!'

The water gurgled out and splashed on the ground under the van. Timmy pricked up his ears and listened. He could see that he would have to get used to quite a lot of new noises here!

'Got your torch?' said Anne when at last they had both got into their bunks. 'I'm going to blow out the lamp. If you want anything in the night you'll have to put on your torch, George. Look at Timmy sitting on the floor still! He doesn't realise we've gone to bed! Tim – are you waiting for us to go upstairs?'

Timmy thumped his tail on the floor. That was just exactly what he *was* waiting for. When George went to bed she *always* went upstairs, whether she was at school or at home – and though he hadn't managed to discover any stairs in the caravan yet, he was sure that George knew where they were!

It took Timmy a few minutes to realise that George was going to sleep for the night in the bunk she had put up against the wall. Then, with one bound he was on top of her, and settled down on her legs. She gave a groan.

'Oh, Timmy – you *are* rough! Get off my legs – get further down – get into the curve of my knees.'

Timmy found the bunk too small to be really comfortable. However he managed to curl himself up in as small a space as possible, put his head down on one of George's knees, gave one of his heavy sighs, and fell asleep.

He had one ear open all the time, though – an ear for a rat that for some peculiar reason ran over the roof – an ear for a daring rabbit that nibbled the grass under the caravan – and a very alert ear for a big cockchafer that flew straight into the glass pane of the right-hand window, just above George's bunk.

Plang! It collided with the pane, and fell back, stunned. Timmy couldn't for the life of him think what it was, but soon fell asleep again, still with one ear open. The blackbird in the hawthorn tree woke him up early. It had thought of a perfectly new melody, and was trying it out very loudly and deliberately. A thrush nearby joined in.

'Mind how you do it, mind how you do it!' sang the thrush at the top of its voice. Timmy sat up and stretched. George woke up at once, because Timmy trod heavily on her middle.

She couldn't think where she was at first, then she remembered and smiled. Of course – in a caravan, with Anne. How that blackbird sang – a better song than the thrush! Cows mooed in the distance, and the early morning sun slid in through the window and picked out the clock and the bowl of primroses.

Timmy settled down. If George wasn't going to get up neither was he! George shut her eyes and fell asleep again too. Outside, the camp began to awake. Caravan doors opened. Fires were lit. Somebody went down to the stream to get water.

The boys came banging at the door of the girls' caravan. 'Come on, sleepyheads! It's half past seven, and we're hungry!'

'Goodness!' said Anne, sitting up, bright-eyed with sleep. 'George! Wake up!'

It wasn't long before they were all sitting round a little fire, from which came a very nice smell. Dick was frying bacon and eggs, and the smell made everyone very hungry. Anne had boiled a kettle on her little stove, and made some tea. She came down the steps with a tray on which she had put the teapot and hot water.

'Anne always does things properly,' said Dick. 'Here, hold your plate out, Ju – your bacon's done. Take your nose out of the way, Timmy, you silly dog – you'll get it splashed with hot fat again. Do look after Timmy when I'm cooking, George. He's already wolfed one slice of bacon.'

'Well, it saved you cooking it,' said George. 'I say, aren't there a lot of caravans here now? They must have come last night.'

They stared round at the field. Besides the snake-man's caravan, and Bufflo's and Mr India-rubber's, there were four or five more.

One interested the children very much. It was a brilliant yellow with red flames painted on the sides. The name on it was 'Alfredo, the Fire-Eater'.

'I imagine him to be a great big, fierce chap,' said Dick. 'A regular fire-eater, with a terribly ferocious temper, an enormous voice and a great stride when he walks.'

'He will probably be a skinny little fellow who trots along like a pony,' said Julian.

'There's someone coming out of his caravan now,' said George. 'Look.'

'It's a woman,' said Anne. 'His wife, I expect. How tiny she is – rather sweet. She looks Spanish.'

'*This* must be the fire-eater, coming behind her,' said George. 'Surely it is! And he's JUST like you imagined him, Dick. How clever of you!'

A great big fellow came down the steps behind his tiny wife. He certainly looked very fierce, for he had a lion-like mane of tawny hair, and a big red face with large, gleaming eyes. He took enormous strides as he went, and his wife had to run to keep up with him.

'*Just* my idea of a fire-eater,' said Dick, pleased. 'I think we'll keep out of his way until we know if he also dislikes children, like the snake-man. What a tiny wife he has! I bet he makes her run around him, and wait on him hand and foot.'

'Well, he's fetching water from the stream for her, anyway,' said Anne. 'Two huge pails. My word, he really does look like a fire-eater, doesn't he?'

'There's somebody else, look,' said Dick. 'Now who would *he* be? Look at him going to the stream – he walks like a tiger or a cat – all slinky and powerful.'

'The man who can set himself free from ropes no matter how he's tied!' said Anne. 'I'm sure he is.'

It was most exciting to watch the new arrivals. They all seemed to know one another. They stopped to talk, they laughed, they visited one another's caravans, and finally three of the women set off together with baskets.

'Going off to shop,' said Anne. 'That's what *I* ought to do. Coming, George? There's a bus that goes down to the village in about ten minutes. We can easily clear up when we come back.'

'Right,' said George, and got up too. 'What are the boys going to do while we're gone?'

'Oh, fetch more water, find sticks for the fire, and see to their own bunks,' said Anne, airily.

'Are we *really*?' said Dick, grinning. 'Well, we might. On the other hand, we might not. Anyway, you two go, because food is getting rather low. A very serious thought, that! Anne, get me some more toothpaste, will you? And if you can spot some of those doughnuts at the dairy, bring a dozen back with you.'

'Yes – and see if you can get a tin of pineapple,' said Julian. 'Don't forget we want milk too.'

'If you want many more things you'll have to come and help us carry them,' said Anne. 'Anything else?'

'Call at the post office and see if there are any letters,' said Dick. 'And don't forget to buy a paper. We may as well find out if anything has happened in the outside world! Not that I feel I can take much interest in it at the moment.'

'Right,' said Anne. 'Come on, George – we shall miss that bus!' And off they went with Timmy at their heels.

CHAPTER SIX

Unfriendly folk

THE TWO boys decided they *would* fetch the water and stack up some firewood while the girls were gone. They 'made' their bunks too, by the simple process of dragging off all the clothes and bundling them on the shelf, and then letting down the bunks against the wall.

That done there didn't seem much else to do except wait for the girls. So they took a walk round the field. They kept a good distance from the snake-man, who was doing something peculiar to one of his pythons.

'It *looks* as if he's polishing it, but he surely can't be,' said Julian. 'I'd like to go near enough to watch but he's such a hot-tempered little fellow he might quite well set one of those enormous pythons on to us!'

The snake-man was sitting on a box, with one snake spread over his knee, some of its coils round one of his legs, the other coils round his waist. The head appeared to be under his armpit. The man was rubbing away hard at the snake's scaly body, and it really seemed as if the python was enjoying it!

Bufflo was doing something with a whip. It had a magnificent handle, set with semi-precious stones that caught the sun and glittered in many colours.

'Look at the lash,' said Julian. 'Yards and yards long! I'd like to see him crack it!'

Almost as if he heard him, Bufflo got to his feet, and swung the great whip in his hand. Then he raised it – and a moment later there was a sound exactly like a pistol-shot! The lash cracked as it was whipped through the air, and the two boys jumped, not expecting such a loud noise.

Bufflo cracked it again. Then he whistled and a small plump woman came to the steps of his caravan.

'You mended it yet?' she called.

'Perhaps,' said Bufflo. 'Get a cigarette, Skippy. Hurry!'

Skippy put her hand into the caravan, felt along a shelf, and brought out a packet of cigarettes. She didn't go down the steps, but stood there, holding out the cigarette between her finger and thumb.

Bufflo swung his whip. CRACK! The cigarette disappeared as if by magic! The boys stared in amazement. Surely the end of the lash hadn't whipped that cigarette from Skippy's fingers? It didn't seem possible.

'There it is,' said Bufflo, pointing some distance away. 'Hold it again, Skippy. I reckon this whip is OK now.'

Skippy picked up the cigarette and put it in her mouth!

'No!' called Bufflo. 'I ain't sure enough of this lash yet. You hold it like you did.'

Skippy took it out of her mouth and held out the cigarette in her finger and thumb once more.

CRACK! Like a pistol-shot the whip cracked again, and once more the cigarette disappeared.

'Aw, Bufflo – you've gone and broken it in half,' said Skippy, reproachfully, pointing to where it lay on the ground, neatly cut in half. 'That was real careless of you.'

Bufflo said nothing. He merely turned his back on Skippy, and set to work on his lash again, though what he was doing neither of the boys could make out. They went a little nearer to see.

Bufflo had his back to them but he must have heard them coming. 'You clear out,' he said, hardly raising his voice. 'No kids allowed round here. Clear out – or I'll crack my whip and take the top hairs off your head!'

Julian and Dick felt perfectly certain he would be

able to carry out his threat, and they retreated with as much dignity as they could. 'I suppose the snake-man told him what a disturbance old Timmy made yesterday with the snakes,' said Dick. 'I hope it won't spoil things for us with all the fair-folk.'

They went across the field and on the way met Mr India-rubber. They couldn't help staring at him. He honestly looked as if he were made of rubber – he was a curious grey, the grey of an ordinary school rubber, and his skin looked rubbery too.

He scowled at the two boys. 'Clear out,' he said. 'No kids allowed in our field.'

Julian was annoyed. 'It's our field as much as yours,' he said. 'We've got a couple of caravans here – those over there.'

'Well, this has always *been* our field,' said Mr India-rubber. 'So you clear out to the next one.'

'We haven't any horses to pull our caravans, even if we wanted to go, which we don't,' retorted Julian, angrily. 'Anyway, why should you object to us? We'd like to be friendly. We shan't do you any harm, or make a nuisance of ourselves.'

'Us-folk and you-folk don't mix,' said the man, obstinately. 'We don't want you here – nor them posh caravans down there, neither,' and he pointed to the

49

three modern caravans in one corner of the field. 'This has always been *our* field.'

'Don't let's argue about it,' said Dick, who had been looking at the man with the greatest curiosity. 'Are you really so rubbery that you can wriggle in and out of pipes and things? Do you—'

But he didn't have time to finish his question because the rubber-man flung himself down on the ground, did a few strange contortions, flicked himself between the boys' legs – and there they both were, flat on the ground! The rubber-man was walking off, looking quite pleased with himself.

'Well!' said Dick, feeling a bump on his head. 'I tried to grab his legs and they honestly felt like rubber! I say – what a pity these people resent us being in their field. It's not going to be very pleasant to have them all banded against us. Not fair either. I should *like* to be friendly.'

'Well, perhaps it's just a case of us-folk and you-folk,' said Julian. 'There's a lot of that kind of feeling about these days, and it's so silly. We're all the same under the skin. We've always got on well with anyone before.'

They hardly liked to go near the other caravans, though they longed to have a closer view of Alfredo the Fire-Eater.

'He looked so *exactly* like what I imagined a fire-eater ought to be,' said Dick. 'I should think he's probably chief of all the fair-folk here – if they've got a chief.'

'Look – here he comes!' said Julian. And sure enough, round the corner came Alfredo, running fast. He came towards the boys, and Julian at first thought that he was coming to chase them away. He didn't mean to run from Alfredo, but it wasn't very pleasant standing still, either, with this enormous fellow racing towards them, his cheeks as red as fire, his great mane of hair flopping up and down.

And then they saw why Alfredo was running! After him came his wife. She was shrieking at him in another language, and was chasing him with a saucepan!

Alfredo lumbered by the two boys, looking scared out of his life. He went down to the stile, leapt over it and disappeared down the lane.

The woman watched him go. When he turned to look round she waved the saucepan at him.

'Big bad one!' she cried. 'You burn breakfast again! Again, again! I bang you with saucepan, big bad one. Come, Alfredo, come!'

But Alfredo had no intention of coming. The angry

woman turned to the two boys. 'He burn breakfast,' she said. 'He no watch, he burn always.'

'It seems odd for a fire-eater to burn something he's cooking,' said Julian. 'Though, on second thoughts, perhaps it's not!'

'Poof! Fire-eating, it is easy!' said Alfredo's hot-tempered wife. 'Cooking is not so easy. It needs brains and eyes and hands. But Fredo, he has no brains, his hands are clumsy – he can only eat fire, and what use is that?'

'Well – I suppose he makes money by it,' said Dick, amused.

'He is my big bad one,' said the woman. She turned to go and then turned back again with a sudden smile. 'But he is very good sometimes,' she said.

She went back to her caravan. The boys looked at one another. 'Poor Alfredo,' said Dick. 'He looks as brave as a lion, and he's certainly a giant of a man – but he's as timid as a mouse. Fancy running away from that tiny woman.'

'Well, I'm not so sure I wouldn't too, if she came bounding over the field after me, brandishing that dangerous-looking saucepan,' said Julian. 'Ah – who's this?'

The man that Anne had thought might be the one

who could set himself free when bound with ropes was coming up from the stile. He walked easily and lightly, really very like a cat. Julian glanced at his hands – they were small but looked very strong. Yes – he could certainly undo knots with hands like that. They gazed at him curiously.

'No kids allowed here,' said the man, as he came up.

'Sorry, but we're caravanners too,' said Dick. 'I say – are you the fellow that can undo ropes when he's tied up in them?'

'Could be,' said the man, and walked on. He turned round suddenly. 'Like me to tie *you* up?' he called. 'I've a good mind to try. Don't you try interfering with us, or I'll do it!'

'Dear me – what a nice, pleasant lot they are!' said Julian. 'Quite different from the other circus folk we've known. I begin to feel we shan't make friends as fast as I thought!'

'We'd better be careful, I think,' said Dick. 'They seem to resent us, goodness knows why. They may make things jolly unpleasant. Don't let's snoop round any more this morning. Let's keep away from them till they get a bit used to us. Then perhaps they'll be more friendly.'

'We'll go and meet the girls,' said Julian. So they went

down to the stile and walked to the bus stop. The bus came panting up the hill at that very moment, and the girls stepped off, with the three fair-women behind them.

The girls joined the boys. 'We've done a lot of shopping,' said Anne. 'Our baskets are awfully heavy. Thanks, Julian, if you'll carry mine. Dick can take George's. Did you see those women who got off with us?'

'Yes,' said Julian. 'Why?'

'Well, we tried to talk to them but they were very unfriendly,' said Anne. 'We felt quite uncomfortable. And Timmy growled like anything, of course, which made things worse. I don't think he liked the smell of them.'

'*We* didn't get on too well either, with the rest of the fair-folk,' said Julian. 'In fact I can't say that Dick and I were a success at all. All they wanted us to do was to clear out.'

'I got a paper for you,' said Anne, 'and George found a letter at the post office from her mother. It's addressed to all of us so we didn't open it. We'll read it when we get to the caravans.'

'I *hope* it's nearly time for dinner,' said George. 'What do *you* think, Timmy?'

UNFRIENDLY FOLK

Timmy knew the word dinner! He gave a joyful bark and led the way. Dinner? There couldn't be a better idea!

CHAPTER SEVEN

A letter – a walk – and a shock

GEORGE OPENED her mother's letter when they had finished their meal. Everyone voted that it was a truly wizard lunch – two hard-boiled eggs each, fresh lettuce, tomatoes, mustard and cress, and potatoes baked in the fire in their jackets – followed by what Julian had asked for – slices of tinned pineapple, very sweet and juicy.

'Very nice,' said Julian, lying back in the sun. 'Anne, you're a jolly good housekeeper. Now, George, let's hear what Aunt Fanny has got to say in her letter.'

George unfolded the notepaper and smoothed it out. 'It's to all of us,' she said.

'DEAR GEORGE, ANNE, JULIAN and DICK,

'I hope George arrived safely and that you all met her. I am really writing to remind George that it is her grandmother's birthday on Saturday, and she must write to her. I forgot to remind George before she went, so thought I must quickly send a letter.

'George, your father is very much upset to read about those two missing scientists. He knows Derek Terry-Kane very well, and worked with him for some time. He says he is absolutely sure that he isn't a traitor to his country; he thinks he has been spirited away somewhere, and Jeffrey Pottersham too – probably in a plane miles away by now, in a country that will force them to give up their secrets. It's just as well you went off today, because this afternoon your father is striding about all over the place, talking nineteen to the dozen, and banging every door he comes to, bless him.

'If you write, please don't mention scientists, as I am hoping he will calm down soon. He really is very upset, and keeps on saying, "What is the world coming to?" when he knows quite well that it's coming to exactly what the scientists plan it to come to.

'Have a good time, all of you, and DON'T forget to write to your grandmother, George!

'Your loving,

MOTHER (AUNT FANNY).'

'I can just see Father striding about like a – like a . . .'

'Fire-eater,' said Julian with a grin, as George stopped for a word. 'He'll drive Aunt Fanny into chasing him around with a saucepan one day! Funny business about these scientists though, isn't it? After all, Terry-Kane *had* planned to leave the country – got his aeroplane ticket and everything – so although your father believes in him, George, it honestly looks a bit fishy, doesn't it?'

'Anything in the paper about it?' asked Dick, and shook it open. 'Yes – here we are:

MISSING SCIENTISTS

It is now certain that Jeffrey Pottersham was in the pay of a country unfriendly to us, and was planning to join Terry-Kane on his journey abroad. Nothing has been heard of the two men, although reports that they have been seen in many places abroad have been received.'

'That rather settles it,' said Julian. 'Two Really Bad Eggs. Look – here are their photographs.'

The four leant over the paper, looking at the pictures of the two men. 'Well, I should have thought *anyone* would recognise Terry-Kane if they saw him,' said Anne. 'Those big, thick, arched eyebrows, and that enormous forehead. If I saw anyone with eyebrows like that I'd think they weren't real!'

A LETTER – A WALK – AND A SHOCK

'He'll shave them off,' said Dick. 'Then he'll look completely different. Probably stick them on his upper lip upside down and use them for moustaches!'

'Don't be silly,' said George, with a giggle. 'The other fellow is very ordinary-looking, except for his dome of a head. Pity none of us four have got great foreheads – I suppose we must be rather stupid people!'

'We're not so bad,' said Julian. 'We've had to use our brains many times in all our adventures – and we haven't come off so badly!'

'Let's clear up and then go for a walk again,' said Anne. 'If we don't I shall fall asleep. This sun is so gloriously hot, it's really cooking me.'

'Yes – we'd better go for a walk,' said Julian, getting up. 'Shall we go and see the castle, do you think? Or shall we leave that for another day?'

'Leave it,' said Anne. 'I honestly don't feel like clambering up that steep hill just now. I think the morning would be a better time!'

They cleared up and then locked the two caravans and set out. Julian looked back. Some of the fair-folk were sitting together, eating a meal. They watched the children in silence. It wasn't very pleasant somehow.

'They don't exactly love us, do they?' said Dick. 'Now you listen, Timmy – don't you go accepting any titbits from people here, see?'

'Oh, Dick!' said George, in alarm. 'You surely don't think they would harm Timmy?'

'No, I don't really,' said Dick. 'But we might as well be careful. As the rubber-man pointed out to us this morning, us-folk and his-folk think differently about some things. It just can't be helped. But I do wish they'd let us be friendly. I don't like this kind of thing.'

'Well, anyway, I shall keep Timmy to heel all the time,' said George, making up her mind firmly. 'Timmy, to heel!' Please understand that as long as we are in the caravan field you must walk to heel! *Do* you understand?'

'Woof-woof,' said Timmy, and immediately kept so close to George's ankles that his nose kept bumping into them.

They decided to catch the bus to Tinkers' Green, and then walk from there to the sea. They would have time to get there and back before dark. The bus was waiting at the corner, and they ran to catch it. It was about two miles to Tinkers' Green, which was a dear little village, with a proper green and a duck-pond with white ducks swimming on it.

'Shall we have an ice-cream?' suggested Dick as they

came to a grocer's shop with an ice-cream sign outside it.

'No,' said Julian firmly. 'We've just had an enormous lunch, and we'll save up ice-cream for tea-time. We shall never get down to the sea if we sit and eat ice-creams half the afternoon!'

It was a lovely walk, down violet-studded lanes, and then over a heathery common with clumps of primroses in the hollows – and even a few very, very early bluebells, much to Anne's delight.

'There's the sea! Oh, what a dear little bay!' said Anne, in delight. 'And isn't it blue – as blue as cornflowers. We could almost bathe.'

'You wouldn't like it if you did,' said Julian. 'The sea would be as cold as ice! Come on – let's get down to the little jetty and have a look at the fishing boats.'

They went down to the sun-warmed stone jetty and began talking to the fishermen there. Some were sitting in the sun mending their nets, and were very willing to talk.

'How nice to have a bit of friendliness shown us instead of the stares and rudeness of the fair-folk!' said Dick to Julian, who nodded and agreed.

A fisherman took them on his boat, and explained a lot of things they already knew and some they didn't. It was nice to sit and listen to his broad speech, and to watch his bright blue eyes as he talked. He was as tanned as an oak-apple.

'Could we ever hire a boat here if we wanted to?' asked Julian. 'Is there one we could manage by ourselves? We are quite good at sailing.'

'Old Joseph there has a boat he could hire out if you wanted one,' said the man they were talking to. 'He hired it out the other day, and I expect he'd hire it out to you too if you think you can really manage it.'

'Thanks. We'll ask him, if we ever decide to go out,' said Julian. He looked at his watch. 'We'd better go and get some tea somewhere. We want to be home before dark. We're camping over at Faynights Castle.'

'Oh ay?' said the fisherman. 'You've got the fair-folk there now, haven't you? They were here two weeks since. My, that fire-eater is a fair treat, he is! And that rope-man – well! I tell you this – I tied him up in my fishing-line – you can see it here, strong as two ropes it is! I tied him up with all the knots I know – and in under a minute he stood up and the line fell off him, knots and all!'

'Ay, that is so,' said the old fellow called Joseph. 'A wonder he is, that man. So is the rubber fellow. He called for a drainpipe, narrow as this, see? And he wriggled through it, quick as an eel. Fair scared me, it did, to see him wriggling out of the other end.'

'We'll go and see them perform when they begin their show,' said Julian. 'At the moment they're not very friendly towards us. They don't like us being in their field.'

'They keeps themselves to themselves,' said Joseph. 'They had a heap of trouble at the place they were in before they came to us – someone set the police on them, and now they won't make friends with anyone.'

'Well, we must go,' said Julian, and they said goodbye to the friendly fishermen and went. They stopped and had tea at a little teashop, and then made their way home. 'Anyone want to take the bus?' said Julian. 'We can easily get home before dark if we walk – but if the girls are tired we'll bus from Tinkers' Green.'

'Of *course* we're not tired!' said George, indignantly. 'Have you *ever* known me say I'm tired, Julian?'

'All right, all right – it was just a bit of politeness on my part,' said Julian. 'Come on – let's get going.'

The way was longer than they had thought. It was getting dark when they got to the stile that led into the caravan field. They climbed over it and made their way slowly to their corner.

And then they suddenly stopped and stared. They looked all round and stared again.

Their two caravans were gone! They could see the places where they had stood, and where their fire had been. But no caravans stood there now!

'*Well!*' said Julian, astounded. 'This beats everything! Are we dreaming? I can't see a sign of our caravans anywhere!'

'Yes – but – *how* could they go?' said Anne, almost stammering in her surprise. 'I mean – we had no horses to pull them away anywhere! They couldn't go just by themselves.'

There was a silence. The four were completely bewildered. How could two large, solid caravans disappear into thin air?

'Look – there are wheel-marks in the grass,' said Dick suddenly. 'See – our caravans went this way – come on, follow. Down the hillside, look!'

In the greatest astonishment the four children and Timmy followed the wheel-marks. Julian glanced back once, feeling that they were being watched. But not one of the fair-folk was to be seen. 'Perhaps they are watching silently behind their caravan curtains,' Julian thought, uncomfortably.

The wheel-marks went right down the field and reached the gate. It was shut now, but it must have been opened for the two caravans, because there were marks

64

in the grass by the gate, marks that passed through it and then were lost in the lane.

'What are we to do?' said Anne, scared. 'They're gone! We've nowhere to sleep. Oh, Julian – what are we going to *do*?'

CHAPTER EIGHT

Where are the caravans?

FOR ONCE in a way Julian was quite at a loss what to do! It looked as if someone had stolen the two caravans – taken them right away somewhere!

'I suppose we'd better ring up the police,' he said. 'They'll watch out for the two caravans, and arrest the thieves. But that won't help us much for tonight! We've got to find somewhere to sleep.'

'I think we ought to go and tackle one or two of the fair-folk,' said Dick. 'Even if they have got nothing to do with the theft they *must* have seen the caravans being taken away.'

'Yes. I think you're right,' said Julian. 'They must know *something* about it. George, you stay here with Anne, in case the fair people are rude. We'll take Timmy – he may be useful!'

George didn't want to stay behind – but she could see that Anne did! So she stayed with her, straining her eyes after the two boys as they went back up the hill with Timmy close behind.

'Don't let's go to the snake-man,' said Dick. 'He might be playing with his snakes in his caravan!'

'What possible game can you play with snakes?' said Julian. 'Or are you thinking of snakes and ladders?'

'Funny joke,' said Dick, politely. 'Look – there's somebody by a camp-fire – Bufflo, I think. No, it's Alfredo. Well, we know he isn't as fierce as he looks – let's tackle *him* about the caravans.'

They went up to the big fire-eater, who was sitting smoking by the fire. He didn't hear them coming and jumped violently when Julian spoke to him.

'Mr Alfredo,' began Julian, 'could you tell us where our two caravans have gone? We found them missing when we got back just now.'

'Ask Bufflo,' said Alfredo, gruffly, not looking at them.

'But don't *you* know anything about them?' persisted Julian.

'Ask Bufflo,' said Alfredo, blowing out clouds of smoke. Julian and Dick turned away, annoyed, and went over to Bufflo's caravan. It was shut. They knocked on the door, and Bufflo appeared, his mop of golden hair gleaming in the lamplight.

'Mr Bufflo,' began Julian politely again, 'Mr Alfredo told us to come and ask you about our caravans, which are missing, and . . .'

'Ask the rubber-man,' said Bufflo, shortly, and slammed the door. Julian was angry. He knocked again. The window opened and Skippy, Bufflo's wife, looked out.

'You go and ask Mr India-rubber,' she called, and shut the window with what sounded suspiciously like a giggle.

'Is this a silly trick they're playing on us?' said Dick fiercely.

'Looks like it,' said Julian. 'Well, we'll try the rubber-man. Come on. He's the last one we'll try, though!'

They went to the rubber-man's caravan, and rapped smartly on the door. 'Who's there?' came the voice of Mr India-rubber.

'Come out – we want to ask you something,' said Julian.

'Who's there?' said the rubber-man again.

'You know jolly well who we are,' said Julian, raising his voice. 'Our caravans have been stolen, and we want to find out who took them. If you won't give us any help, we're going to telephone the police.'

The door opened and the rubber-man stood on the top of the steps, looking down at Julian. 'Nobody has stolen them,' he said. 'Nobody at all. You go and ask the snake-man.'

'If you think we're going round asking every single person in this camp, you're mistaken!' said Julian, angrily. 'I don't *want* to go to the police – we wanted to be friends with you fair-folk, not enemies. This is all very silly. If the caravans *are* stolen we've no choice but to go to the police – and I don't imagine you want them after you again! We know they were put on to you a few weeks back.'

'You know too much,' said the rubber-man, in a very surly voice. 'Your caravans are *not* stolen. I will show you where they are.'

He came lightly down the steps of his caravan and walked in front of the two boys in the half-darkness. He went across the grassy hillside, making for where the children's caravans had stood.

'Where are you taking us?' called Julian. 'We know the vans are not there! Please don't act the idiot – there's been enough of that already.'

The man said nothing, but walked on. The boys and Timmy could do nothing but follow. Timmy was not happy. He kept up a continuous low growling, like far-off thunder. The rubber-man took not the slightest notice. Julian wondered idly if he didn't fear dogs because they wouldn't be able to bite rubber!

FIVE HAVE A WONDERFUL TIME

The man took them to the hedge that ran at one side
of the field, beyond where the two caravans had stood.
Julian began to feel exasperated. He knew perfectly
well that the two vans had been taken down to the
field-gate and out into the lane – so why was this fellow
leading them in the opposite direction?

The rubber-man forced his way through the hedge,
and the boys followed – and there, just the other side,
two big, dark shapes loomed up in the twilight – the
caravans!

'Well!' said Julian, taken aback. 'What *was* the idea
of putting the caravans here, in the next field?'

'Us-folk and you-folk don't mix,' said the man. 'We
don't like kids messing about. Three weeks ago we had
a canary-man, with over a hundred canaries that gave a
show with him – and some kids opened all the cages one
night and set them loose.'

'Oh,' said Julian. 'They'd die, of course, if they were
set loose – they don't know how to look for their
own food. That was bad luck. But *we* don't do things
like that.'

'No kids allowed with us now,' said the rubber-man.
'That's why we put horses into your vans, took them
down to the field-gate, and up into the next field –
and here they are. We thought you'd be back in the

daylight and would see them.'

'Well, it's nice to find you can be chatty, all of a sudden,' said Julian. 'Don't growl any more, Timmy. It's all right. We've found our vans!'

The rubber-man disappeared without another word. They heard him squeezing easily through the hedge. Julian took out the key to his caravan, went up the steps and opened the door. He rummaged about and found his torch. He switched it on and shone it round. Nothing had been disturbed.

'Well – so that's that,' he said. 'Just a bit of spite on the part of the fair-folk, I suppose – punishing us for what those horrid kids did to the canaries. I must say it was a shame to open those cages – half the poor little creatures must have died. I don't *like* birds put in cages – but canaries can't live in this country unless they are looked after, it's cruel to let them go loose, and starve.'

'I agree with you,' said Dick. They were now walking down the hillside to a gap in the hedge through which the vans must have been pulled up the hill. George and Anne would be most relieved to hear they had found the caravans!

Julian gave a whistle, and George answered it at once. 'We're still here, Julian! What's happened?'

'We've got the caravans,' shouted back Julian, cheerily. 'They're in this field.'

The girls joined them at once, most surprised to hear this news. Julian explained.

'The fair-folk really have got a hate on against children,' he said. 'Apparently they had a canary-man, whose show consisted of singing canaries – and some kids set all the birds loose one night – so half of them died. And now the fair-folk won't have children anywhere near them.'

'I suppose the snake-man is afraid of us setting his snakes loose,' said Dick, with a chuckle. 'Well, thank goodness we've found the vans. I had a feeling we might have to sleep in a haystack tonight!'

'I wouldn't have minded that,' said George. 'I like haystacks.'

'We'll light a fire and cook something,' said Julian. 'I feel hungry after all this upset.'

'I don't,' said Anne. 'I hate feeling that the fair-folk won't be friends. It's silly of them. We're not used to that.'

'Yes – but they're rather like children themselves,' said Julian. 'Somebody does something unkind to them, so they get sulky, and wait for a chance to hit back – and then someone set the police on them, too, don't forget – they're very touchy at the moment, I imagine.'

WHERE ARE THE CARAVANS?

'Well, it's a pity,' said George, watching Dick light a camp-fire very efficiently. 'I was looking forward to having a good time with them. Do you suppose the farmer will mind us being here?'

'Oh – I never thought of that.' said Julian. 'This may not be a camping field. I hope to goodness we don't have an angry farmer shouting at us tomorrow!'

'And, oh dear, we are so far away from the stream now,' said Anne. 'It's on the other side of the field where we were – and we do badly want water.'

'We'll have to do without it tonight,' said Dick firmly. 'I don't want the top of my hair taken off by Bufflo, or a rope tying up my legs, thrown by the rope-man, or a snake wriggling after me. I bet those fair-folk will be on the watch for us to fetch water. This is all very silly.'

They had rather a solemn meal. Things had suddenly begun to seem rather complicated. They *couldn't* go to the police about such a silly thing – nor did they want to. But if the farmer wanted to turn them out of this field, how could they go back to their first camping place? Nobody wanted to live in a camp surrounded by enemies!

'We'll sleep on it,' said Julian, at last. 'Don't worry, you girls. We'll find a way out of this problem. We are pretty good at getting out of difficulties. Never say die!'

'Woof,' said Timmy, agreeing heartily. George patted him.

'That's one of *your* mottoes, isn't it, Timmy?' she said.

'And another motto of his is "Let sleeping dogs lie",' said Dick, with a broad grin. 'He hates being woken up when he's having a nice nap, dreaming of millions of rabbits to catch!'

'Well, talking of naps, what about getting into our bunks?' said Julian, with a yawn. 'We've had a good long walk today, and I'm tired. I'm going to lie in my bunk and read.'

Everyone thought this a very good idea. They cleared up the supper things, and the girls said good night to the boys. They went into the caravan with Timmy.

'I do hope this holiday isn't going to be a failure,' said Anne, as she got into her bunk. George gave one of her snorts.

'A failure! You wait and see! I've a feeling it will turn out to be *super*.'

CHAPTER NINE

A great surprise

IT DIDN'T seem as if George's feeling that the holiday was going to be 'super' was at all correct the next morning. A loud rapping came on the door of the boys' caravan before they were even awake!

Then a large, red face looked in at the window, startling Julian considerably.

'Who gave you permission to camp here?' said the face, looking as dark as thunder.

Julian went to the door in his pyjamas. 'Do you own this field?' he said, politely. 'Well, we were camping in the next field, and . . .'

'That's let for campers and caravanners,' said the man, who was dressed like a farmer. 'This isn't.'

'As I said, we were in the next field,' repeated Julian, 'and for some reason the fair-folk there didn't like us – and when we were out they brought our caravans here! As we've no horses to take them away, we couldn't do anything else but stay!'

'Well, you *can't* stay,' said the farmer. 'I don't let out

this field. I use it for my cows. You'll have to go today, or I'll put your caravans out into the road.'

'Yes, but look here . . .' began Julian, and then stopped. The farmer had walked off, a determined figure in riding-breeches and tweed coat. The girls opened their window and called to Julian.

'We heard what he said. Isn't he mean? *Now* what are we going to do?'

'We're going to get up and have breakfast,' said Julian. 'And then I'm going to give the fair-folk one more chance – they'll have to lend us two horses – and pull us back into our rightful place. Otherwise I very much fear I shall have to get help from the police!'

'Oh, dear,' said Anne. 'I do hate this kind of thing. We were having such a lovely time before the fair people arrived. But it seems quite impossible to get them to be friends with us.'

'Quite,' said Julian. 'I'm not so sure *I* want to be friendly now, either. I'd rather give up this holiday altogether and go back home than have continual trouble going on round us! Dick and I will go and tackle the fair-folk after breakfast.'

Breakfast was just as solemn as supper had been. Julian was rather silent. He was thinking what was best to say to the sullen folk in the next field. 'You must take

76

Timmy with you,' said George, voicing the thoughts of everyone.

Julian and Dick set off with Timmy about half past eight. All the fair people were up and about, and the smoke of their fires rose up in the morning air.

Julian thought he would go and tackle the fire-eater, so the two boys went towards his caravan. The other fair people looked up, and one by one left their vans or their fires and closed round the boys. Timmy bared his teeth and growled.

'Mr Alfredo,' began Julian, 'the farmer is turning us out of that field. We must come back here. We want you to lend us two horses for our vans.'

A ripple of laughter spread through the listening people. Mr Alfredo answered politely, with a large smile on his face. 'What a pity! We don't hire out our horses!'

'I don't want to hire them from you,' said Julian, patiently. 'It's up to you to let us have them to bring back our vans. Otherwise – well, I shall *have* to go and ask the police for help. Those caravans don't belong to us, you know.'

There was an angry murmur from the listening crowd. Timmy growled more loudly. One or two of the fair-folk stepped back hurriedly when they heard him.

CRACK! Julian turned quickly. The fair people ran back, and the two boys found that they were facing Bufflo, who, with a large and unpleasant grin on his face, was swinging his whip in his hand.

CRACK! Julian jumped violently, for a few hairs from the top of his head were suddenly whisked off into the air – the end of the lash had neatly cut them away!

The crowd laughed loudly. Timmy bared his white teeth, and snarled.

Dick put his hand down on the dog's collar. 'Do that again and I shan't be able to hold the dog!' he called, warningly.

Julian stood there, at a loss to know what to do next. He couldn't *bear* turning tail and going off to the accompaniment of jeers and howls. He was so full of rage that he couldn't say a word.

And then something happened. Something so utterly unexpected that nobody did anything at all except let it happen!

A boyish figure came running up the grass hillside – someone very like George, with short curly hair and a very freckled face – someone dressed, however, in a short grey skirt, and not in jeans, like George.

She came racing up, yelling at the top of her voice.

A GREAT SURPRISE

'Dick! DICK! Hey, DICK!'

Dick turned and stared in amazement.

'Why – it's Jo! JO! The traveller girl who once got mixed up with us in an adventure! Julian, it's Jo!'

There was no doubt about it at all. It *was* Jo! She came tearing up, her face glowing with the utmost delight and flung herself excitedly on Dick. She had always liked him best.

'Dick! I didn't know *you* were here! Julian! Are the others here too? Oh, Timmy, dear old Timmy! Dick, are you camping here? Oh, this is really too marvellous to be true!'

Jo seemed to be about to fling herself on Dick again, and he fended her off. 'Jo! Where in the world have you come from?'

'Well, you see,' said Jo, 'I've got school holidays like you – and I thought I'd go and visit you at Kirrin Cottage. So I did. But you had all gone away together. That was yesterday.'

'Go on,' said Dick, as Jo stopped, out of breath.

'Well, I didn't want to go back home again straight away,' said Jo. 'So I thought I'd pay a visit to my uncle – he's my mother's brother – and I knew he was camping here so I hitchhiked all the way yesterday, and came late last night.'

'Well, I'm blessed,' said Julian. 'And who is your uncle, may I ask?'

'Oh Alfredo – the fire-eater,' was Jo's astonishing reply. 'Didn't you know? Oh, Dick! Oh, Julian! Can I stay here while you're here? Do, DO say I can! You haven't forgotten me, have you?'

'Of course not,' said Dick, thinking that nobody could possibly forget this wild little girl, with her mad ways and her staunch affection.

Then for the first time Jo realised that something was going on! What was this crowd doing round Julian and Dick?

She looked round, and immediately sensed that the fair people were not friendly to the two boys – although the main expression on their faces now was one of astonishment!

How did Jo know these boys? they wondered. How was it she was so very friendly with them? They were puzzled and suspicious.

'Uncle Alfredo, where are you?' demanded Jo, looking all round. 'Oh, there you are! Uncle, these are my very best friends – and so are the girls too, wherever they are. I'll tell you all about them, and how nice they were to me! I'll tell everybody!'

'Well,' said Julian, feeling rather embarrassed at what

Jo might reveal, 'well, you tell them, Jo, and I'll just pop back and break the news to George and Anne. They *will* be surprised to find you are here – and that Alfredo is your uncle!'

The two boys and Timmy turned to go. The little crowd opened to let them pass. It closed up again round the excited Jo, whose high voice the boys could hear all the way across the field.

'Well, well, well!' said Dick, as they got through the hedge. 'What an astonishing thing! I couldn't believe my eyes when young Jo appeared, could you? I hope George won't mind. She was always rather jealous of Jo and the things she could do.'

The two girls were amazed at the boys' news. George was not too pleased. She preferred Jo at a distance rather than near. She liked and admired her but rather unwillingly. Jo was too like George herself for George to give her complete friendliness!

'Well, fancy *Jo*, Jo herself being here!' said Anne, smiling. 'Oh, Julian – it was a good thing she arrived when she did! I don't like that bit about Bufflo cracking his whip at you. He might have made you bald on the top!'

'Oh, it was only a few hairs,' said Julian. 'But it gave me quite a shock. And I think it gave the fair people a shock too when Jo arrived like a little hurricane, yelling at the top of her voice, and flinging herself on poor old Dick. She almost knocked him over!'

'She's not a bad kid,' said Dick, 'but she never stops to think. I wonder if the people she stays with know where she's gone. I wouldn't be a bit surprised if she just disappeared without a word.'

'Like the two scientists,' said Julian, with a grin. 'Gosh, I can't get over it! Jo was the very last person I would expect here.'

'Well, not really, if you think a bit,' said Anne. 'Her father is a traveller, isn't he – and her mother was in a circus, she told us so. She trained dogs, don't you remember, Julian? So it's quite natural for Jo to have relations like the fair people. But just fancy having a fire-eater for an uncle!'

'Yes – I'd forgotten that Jo's mother was in a circus,' said Julian. 'I expect she's got relations all over the country! I wonder what she's telling them about us.'

'She's singing *Dick's* praises anyway,' said George. 'She always thought the world of Dick. Perhaps the fair people won't be *quite* so unfriendly if they know that Jo is fond of us.'

'Well, we're in a bit of a fix,' said Dick. 'We can't stay in this field, or the farmer will be after us again – and I can't see the fair people lending us their horses – and without horses we can't leave this field!'

'We could ask the farmer to lend us his horses,' suggested Anne.

'We'd have to pay him, though, and I don't see why we should,' said Julian. 'After all, it isn't *our* fault that our caravans were moved here.'

'I think this is a horrid and unfriendly place,' said Anne. 'And I don't want to stay here another day. I'm not enjoying it a bit.'

'Cheer up!' said Dick. 'Never say die!'

'Woof,' said Timmy.

'Look – someone's coming through that gap in the hedge down there by the lane,' said George, pointing. 'It's Jo!'

'Yes – and my goodness me, she's got a couple of horses with her!' cried Dick. 'Good old Jo! She's got Alfredo's horses!'

CHAPTER TEN

Back with the fair-folk again

THE FOUR of them, with Timmy capering behind, ran to meet Jo. She beamed at everyone.

'Hallo, Anne, hallo, George! Pleased to meet you again. This isn't half a surprise!'

'Jo! How did you get those horses?' said Dick, taking one by the bridle.

'Easy,' grinned Jo. 'I just told Uncle Fredo all about you – what wonders you were – and all you did for me – and wasn't I shocked when I heard they'd turned you out of your field! I let go then! I told them just what I thought of them, treating my best friends like that!'

'Did you really, Jo?' said George, doubtfully.

'Didn't you hear me?' demanded Jo. 'I yelled like anything at Uncle Fredo, and then his wife, my Aunt Anita, she yelled at him too – and then we both yelled at everyone.'

'It must have been quite a yelling match,' said Julian. 'And the result was that you got your way, and got the horses to take back our caravans, Jo?'

BACK WITH THE FAIR-FOLK AGAIN

'Well, when Aunt Anita told me they'd taken your caravans into the next field and left them there, and wouldn't lend you horses to bring them back, I told them all a few things,' said Jo. 'I said – no, I'd better not tell you what I said. I wasn't very polite.'

'I bet you weren't,' said Dick, who had already had a little experience of Jo's wild tongue the year before.

'And when I told them how my father went to prison, and you got me a home with somebody nice who looks after me, they were sorry they'd treated you roughly,' said Jo. 'And so I told Uncle Fredo I was going to catch two horses and bring your caravans back into the field again.'

'I see,' said Julian. 'And the fair-folk just let you?'

'Oh, yes,' said Jo. 'So let's hitch them in, Julian, and go back at once. Isn't that the farmer coming over there?'

It was, and he looked pretty grim. Julian hurriedly put one horse into the shafts of the girls' caravan, and Dick backed the other horse into the shafts of the second caravan. The farmer came up and watched.

'So you thought you'd get horses after all, did you?' he said. 'I thought you would. Telling me a lot of poppycock about being stranded here and not being able to get away!'

'Grrrrrrrr,' said Timmy at once, but he was the only

one who made any reply!

'Gee-up!' said Jo, taking the reins of the horse pulling the girls' caravan. 'Hup there! Git along, will you?'

The horse got along, and Jo wickedly drove him so near to the farmer that he had to move back in a hurry. He growled something at her. Timmy, appearing round the caravan, growled back. The farmer stood back further, and watched the two caravans going down the hillside, out through the wide gap in the hedge, and down the lane.

They came to the field-gate and Anne opened it. In went the horses, straining now, because they were going uphill, and the vans were heavy. At last they arrived in the corner where the vans had stood before. Julian backed them over the same bit of ground.

He unhitched the horses, and threw the reins of the second horse to Dick. 'We'll take them back ourselves,' he said.

So the two boys walked the horses over to Alfredo, who was pegging up some washing on a line. It seemed a most unsuitable thing for a fire-eater to do, but Alfredo didn't seem to mind.

'Mr Alfredo, thank you for lending us the horses,' said Julian, in his politest tones. 'Shall we tie them up anywhere, or set them loose?'

BACK WITH THE FAIR-FOLK AGAIN

Alfredo turned round, and took some pegs out of his large mouth. He looked rather ashamed.

'Set them loose,' he said. He hesitated before he put the pegs back into his mouth. 'We didn't know you were friends with my niece,' he said. 'She told us all about you. You should have told us you knew her.'

'And how could he do that when he didn't know she was your niece?' shouted Mrs Alfredo from the caravan door. 'Fredo, you have no brains, not a single brain do you have. Ahhhhhh! Now you drop my best blouse on the ground!'

She ran out at top speed, and Alfredo stared in alarm. Fortunately she had no saucepan with her this time. She turned to the two amused boys.

'Alfredo is sorry he took your caravans away,' she said. 'Are you not, Fredo?'

'Well! It was *you* who . . .' began Alfredo, with a look of astonishment. But he wasn't allowed to finish. His wife gave him a violent nudge, and spoke again herself, her words tumbling over one another.

'Pay no attention to this big bad man! He has no brains. He can only eat fire, and that is a poor thing to do! Now, Jo, she has brains. Now, are you not glad that you are back again in your corner?'

'I should have felt gladder if you had all been friendly

to us,' said Julian. 'I'm afraid we don't feel like stopping here any longer, though. We shall probably leave tomorrow.'

'Now there, Fredo, see what you have done! You have chased away these nice children!' cried Mrs Alfredo. 'They have manners, these boys, a thing you know nothing about, Fredo. You should learn from them, Fredo, you should . . .'

Fredo took some pegs from his mouth to make an indignant answer, but his wife suddenly gave a shriek and ran to her caravan. 'Something burns! Something burns!'

Alfredo gave a hearty laugh, a loud guffaw that surprised the boys. 'Ha! She bakes today, and burns her cake! She has no brains, that woman! No brains at all!'

Julian and Dick turned to go. Alfredo spoke to them in a low voice. 'You can stay here now, here in this field. You are Jo's friend. That is enough for us.'

'It may be,' said Julian. 'But it's not quite enough for *us*, I'm afraid. We shall leave tomorrow.'

The boys went back to the caravans. Jo sat on the grass with George and Anne, eagerly telling them of her life with a very nice family. 'But they won't let me wear jeans or be a boy,' she ended sadly. 'That's why I wear a skirt now. Could you lend me some jeans, George?'

'No, I couldn't,' said George, firmly. Jo was quite enough like her as it was, without wearing jeans! 'Well, you seem to have turned over a new leaf, Jo. Can you read and write yet?'

'Almost,' said Jo, and turned her eyes away. She found lessons very difficult, for she had never been to school when she lived with her traveller father. She looked back again with bright eyes. 'Can I stay with you?' she said. 'My foster-mother would let me, I know – if it was you I was with.'

'Didn't you tell her you were coming here?' said Dick. 'That was unkind, Jo.'

'I never thought,' said Jo. 'You send her a card for me, Dick.'

'Send one yourself,' said George at once. 'You said you could write.'

Jo took no notice of that remark. '*Can* I stay with you?' she said. 'I won't sleep in the caravans, I'll doss down underneath. I always did that when the weather was fine, and I lived with my dad in his caravan. It would be a change for me now not to live in a house. I like lots of things in houses, though I never thought I would – but I shall always like sleeping rough best.'

'Well – you *could* stay here with us, if we were going to stay,' said Julian. 'But I don't much feel inclined to, now we've had such an unfriendly welcome from everyone.'

'I'll tell everyone to be kind to you,' said Jo at once, and got up as if she meant to go then and there to force everyone into kindness!

Dick pushed her down. 'No. We'll stay here one more day and night, and make up our minds tomorrow. What do you say, Julian?'

'Right,' said Julian. He looked at his watch. 'Let's go and celebrate Jo's coming with a few ice-creams. And I expect you two girls have got some shopping to do, haven't you?'

'Yes,' said Anne, and fetched the shopping bags. They set off down the hill, the five of them and Timmy. As they passed the snake-man he called out cheerily to them: 'Good morning! Nice day, isn't it?'

After the surliness and sulkiness the children had got from the fair-folk up till then, this came as a surprise. Anne smiled, but the boys and George merely nodded and passed by. They were not so forgiving as Anne!

They passed the rubber-man, bringing back water. Behind him came the rope-man. Both of them nodded to the children, and the sad-looking rubber-man actually gave a brief grin.

Then they saw Bufflo, practising with his whip –

crack- crack-crack! He came over to them. 'If you'd like a crack with my whip, you're welcome any time,' he said to Julian.

'Thanks,' said Julian, politely but stiffly. 'But we're probably leaving tomorrow.'

'Keep your hair on!' said Bufflo, feeling snubbed.

'I would if you'd let me,' said Julian at once, rubbing his hand over the top of his head where Bufflo had stripped off a few up-standing hairs.

'Ho, ho!' guffawed Bufflo and then stopped abruptly, afraid he had given offence. Julian grinned at him. He rather liked Bufflo, with his mop of yellow hair and lazy drawl.

'You stay on with us,' said Bufflo. 'I'll lend you a whip.'

'We're probably leaving tomorrow,' repeated Julian. He nodded to him, and went on with the others.

'I'm beginning to feel I'd rather like to stay after all,' said George. 'It makes such a difference if people are friendly.'

'Well, we're not staying,' said Julian, shortly. 'I've practically made up my mind – but we'll just wait till tomorrow. It's a – matter of pride with me. You girls don't understand quite how I feel about the whole thing.'

They didn't. Dick understood, though, and he agreed with Julian. They went on down to the village and made their way to the ice-cream shop.

They had a very pleasant day. They had a wonderful lunch on the grass by their caravans – and to their surprise Mrs Alfredo presented them with a sponge sandwich she had made. Anne thanked her very much indeed to make up for a certain stiffness in the thanks of the two boys.

'You *might* have said a bit more,' she said reproachfully to them. 'She really is a kind woman. Honestly I wouldn't mind staying on now.'

But Julian was curiously obstinate about it. He shook his head. 'We go tomorrow,' he said. 'Unless something unexpected happens to *make* us stay. And it won't.'

But Julian was quite wrong. Something unexpected *did* happen. Something really very peculiar indeed.

CHAPTER ELEVEN

A very strange thing

THE UNEXPECTED happening came that evening after tea. They had all had rather a late tea, and a very nice one. Bread and butter and honey – new doughnuts from the dairy – and the sponge cake that Mrs Alfredo had presented them with, which had a very rich filling indeed.

'I can't eat a thing more,' said George. 'That sponge cake was too rich for words. I don't even feel as if I can get up and clear away – so don't start suggesting it, Anne.'

'I'm not,' said Anne. 'There's plenty of time. It's a heavenly evening – let's sit for a while. There goes that blackbird again. He has a different tune every time he sings.'

'That's what I like about blackbirds,' said Dick, lazily. 'They're proper composers. They make up their own tunes – not like the chaffinch who just carols the same old song again and again and again. Honestly there was one this morning that said it fifty times without stopping.'

'Chip-chip-chip, cherry-erry-erry, chippee-OO-EE-Ar!' shouted a chaffinch, rattling it all off as if he had learnt it by heart. 'Chip-chip-chip . . .'

'There he goes again,' said Dick. 'If he doesn't say that, he shouts "pink-pink-pink" as if he'd got that colour on the brain. Look at him over there – isn't he a beauty?'

He certainly was. He flew down to the grass beside the children and began to peck up the crumbs, even venturing on to Anne's knee once. She sat still, really thrilled.

Timmy growled, and the chaffinch flew off. 'Silly, Timmy,' said George. 'Jealous of a chaffinch! Oh, look, Dick – are those herons flying down to the marsh on the east side of the castle hill?'

'Yes, said Dick, sitting up. 'Where are your field-glasses, George? We could see the big birds beautifully through them.'

George fetched them from her caravan. She handed them to Dick. He focused them on the marsh. 'Yes – four herons – gosh, what long legs they've got, haven't they? They are wading happily about – now one's struck down at something with its great beak. What's it got? Yes, it's a frog. I can see its back legs!'

A VERY STRANGE THING

'You can't!' said George, taking the field-glasses from him. 'You're a fibber. The glasses aren't powerful enough to see a frog's legs all that way off!'

But they *were* powerful enough. They were really magnificent ones, far too good for George, who wasn't very careful with valuable things.

She was just in time to see the poor frog's legs disappearing into the big, strong beak of the heron. Then something frightened the birds, and before the others could have a look at them they had all flapped away.

'How slowly they flap their wings,' said Dick. 'They must surely flap them more slowly than any other bird. Give me the glasses again, George. I'll have a squint at the jackdaws. There are thousands of them flying again over the castle – their evening jaunt, I suppose.'

He put them to his eyes, and moved the glasses to and fro, watching the endless whirl and swoop of the black jackdaws. The sound of their many voices came loudly over the evening air. 'Chack-chack-chack-chack!'

Dick saw some fly down to the only complete tower of the castle. He lowered the glasses to follow them. One jackdaw flew down to the sill of the slit-window near the top of the tower, and Dick followed its flight. It rested for half a second on the sill and then flew off as if frightened.

And then Dick saw something that made his heart suddenly jump. His glasses were trained on the window-slit and he saw something most astonishing there! He gazed as if he couldn't believe his eyes.

Then he spoke in a low voice to Julian.

'Ju! Take the glasses, will you? Train them on the window-slit near the top of the only complete tower – and tell me if you see what I see. Quick!'

Julian held out his hand in astonishment for the glasses. The others stared in surprise. What could Dick have seen? Julian put the glasses to his eyes and focused them on the window Dick had been looking at. He stared hard.

'Yes. Yes, I can. What an extraordinary thing. It must be an effect of the light, I think.'

By this time the others were in such a state of curiosity that they couldn't bear it. George snatched the glasses from Julian. 'Let *me* see!' she said, quite fiercely. She trained them on to the window. She gazed and gazed and gazed.

Then she lowered the glasses and stared at Julian and Dick. 'Are you being funny?' she said. 'There's nothing there – nothing but an empty window!'

Anne snatched the glasses from her just before Dick tried to take them again. She too trained them on the window. But there was absolutely nothing there to see.

'There's nothing,' said Anne, disgusted, and Dick took the glasses from her at once, focusing them once more on the window. He lowered them.

'It's gone,' he said to Julian. 'Nothing there now.'

'DICK! If you don't tell us what you saw we'll roll you down the hill,' said George, crossly. 'Are you making something up? *What* did you see?'

'Well,' said Dick, looking at Julian. '*I* saw a face. A face not far from the window, staring out. What did you see, Ju?'

'The same,' said Julian. 'It made me feel pretty peculiar, too.'

'A *face*!' said George, Anne and Jo all together. 'What do you mean?'

'Well – just what we said,' replied Dick. 'A face – with eyes and nose and mouth.'

'But nobody lives in the castle. It's a ruin,' said George. 'Was it someone exploring, do you think?'

Julian looked at his watch. 'No, it couldn't have been a visitor, I'm sure – the castle shuts at half past five and it's gone six. Anyway – it looked a – a – sort of *desperate* face!'

'Yes. I thought so too,' said Dick. 'It's – well, it's very peculiar, isn't it, Julian? There may be some kind of ordinary explanation for it, but I can't help feeling there's something *odd* about it.'

'Was it a man's face?' asked George. 'Or a woman's?'

'A man's, I think,' said Dick. 'I couldn't see any hair against the darkness inside the window. Or clothes. But it *looked* a man's face. Did you notice the eyebrows, Ju?'

'Yes, I did,' said Julian. 'They were very pronounced, weren't they?'

This rang a bell with George! 'Eyebrows!' she said at once. 'Don't you remember – the picture of that scientist, Terry-Kane, showed that he had thick black eyebrows – you said he'd shave them off and use them upside down for moustaches, don't you remember, Dick?'

'Yes. I do remember,' said Dick, and looked at Julian. Julian shook his head. 'I didn't recognise the likeness,' he said, 'but after all it's a very long way away. It is only because George's glasses are so extraordinarily good that we managed to spot a face looking out of a window so very far away. Actually I think there will be an ordinary explanation – it's just that we were so startled – and that made us think it was very strange.'

'I *wish* I'd seen the face,' sighed George. 'They're my glasses, too – and I never saw the face!'

'Well, you can keep on looking and see if it comes back,' said Dick, handing over the glasses. 'It may do.'

So Anne, George, and Jo took turn and turn about,

gazing earnestly through the field-glasses – but they saw no face. In the end it got so dark that it was quite difficult to make out the tower, let alone the window or a face!

'I tell you what we might do,' said Julian. 'We could go and see over the castle ourselves tomorrow. And we could go up into that tower. Then we should certainly see if there's a face there.'

'But I thought we were leaving tomorrow,' said Dick.

'Oh – yes, we did think of leaving, didn't we?' said Julian, who had quite forgotten this idea of his in his excitement. 'Well – I don't feel as if we can go before we've explored that castle, and found the explanation of the face.'

'Of *course* we can't,' said George. 'Fancy seeing a thing like that and rushing off without finding out about it. I couldn't possibly.'

'*I'm* going to stay anyhow,' announced Jo. 'I could stop with my Uncle Alfredo, if you go, and I'll let you know if the face comes again – if George will leave me her glasses.'

'Well, I shan't,' said George, with much determination. 'If I go, my glasses go with me. But I'm not going. You *will* stay now, won't you, Julian?'

'We'll stay and find out about the face,' said Julian.

'I honestly feel awfully puzzled about it. Hallo, who's this coming?'

A big figure loomed up in the twilight. It was Alfredo, the fire-eater. 'Jo! Are you there?' he said. 'Your aunt invites you to supper – and all your friends too. Come along.'

There was a pause. Anne looked expectantly across at Julian. Was he still going to be high and mighty and proud? She hoped not.

'Thanks,' said Julian, at last. 'We'd be pleased to come. Do you mean now?'

'That would be nice,' said Alfredo, with a little bow. 'I fire-eat for you? Anything you say!'

This was too tempting to resist. Everyone got up at once and followed the big Alfredo over the hillside to his caravan. Outside there was a really good fire, and on it was a big black pot that gave out a wonderful smell.

'Supper is not quite ready,' said Alfredo. The five children were relieved. After their big tea they didn't feel ready even for a meal that smelt as good as the one in the pot! They sat down by it.

'Will you really eat fire for us?' asked Anne. 'How do you do it?'

'Ah, very difficult!' said Alfredo. 'I do it only if you promise me not to try it by yourselves. You would not like blisters all over your mouth inside, would you?'

Everyone felt certain that they wouldn't. 'I don't want you to have blisters in *your* mouth, either,' added Anne.

Alfredo looked shocked. 'I am a very good fire-eater,' he assured her. 'No good ones ever make blisters in their mouths. Now – you sit still and I will fetch my torch and eat fire for you.'

Someone else sat down beside them. It was Bufflo. He grinned at them. Skippy came and sat down too. Then the snake-man came up, and he sat down on the opposite side of the fire.

Alfredo came back carrying a few things in his hands. 'Quite a family circle!' he said. 'Now watch – I will eat fire for you!'

CHAPTER TWELVE

Fire-eating and other things!

ALFREDO SAT down on the grass, some way back from the fire. He set a little metal bowl in front of him, that smelt of petrol. He held up two things to show the children.

'His torches,' said Mrs Alfredo, proudly. 'He eats fire from them.'

Alfredo called out something to the snake-man, dipping his two torches into the bowl. They were not alight yet, and to the children they looked like very large button-hooks, with a wad of wool caught in the hook part.

The snake-man leant forward and took a burning twig out of the fire. With a deft throw he pitched it right into the metal bowl. Immediately it set light to the petrol there, and flames shot up in the darkness.

Alfredo had held his torches out of the way, but now he thrust first one and then another into the burning petrol in the bowl.

They flared alight at once, and red flames shot up as he held one in each hand. His eyes gleamed in the brilliant light, and the five children sat still, spellbound.

Then Alfredo leant back his head – back and back – and opened his great mouth wide. He put one of the lighted torches into it, and closed his mouth over it, so that his cheeks gleamed a strange and unbelievable red from the flames inside his mouth. Anne gave a little scream and George gasped. The two boys held their breath. Only Jo watched unconcerned. She had seen her uncle do this many times before!

Alfredo opened his mouth, and flames rushed out of it, gushing like a fiery waterfall. What with the other torch flaring in his left hand, the burning petrol in the bowl, the torch in his right hand and the flames from his mouth, it really was an extraordinary scene!

He did the same with the other torch, and once more his cheeks glowed like a lamp. Then fire came from his mouth again, and was blown this way and that by the night breeze.

Alfredo closed his mouth. He swallowed. Then he looked round, opened his mouth to show that he no longer had any flames there, and smiled broadly.

'Ah – you like to see me eat fire?' he said, and put out his torches. The bowl was no longer flaming, and now only the fire light lit the scene.

'It's marvellous,' said Julian, with great admiration.

'But don't you burn your mouth?'

'What me? No, never!' laughed Alfredo. 'At first maybe, yes – when I begin years and years ago. But now, no. It would be a shameful thing to burn my mouth – I would hang my head, and go away.'

'But – how is it you *don't* burn your mouth?' asked Dick, puzzled.

Alfredo refused to give any explanation. That was part of the mystery of his act and he wasn't going to give it away.

'*I* can fire-eat too,' announced Jo, casually and most unexpectedly. 'Here, Uncle, let me have one of your torches.'

'You! You will do nothing of the sort!' roared Alfredo. 'Do you want to burn to bits?'

'No. And I shan't either,' said Jo. 'I've watched you and I know just how it's done. I've tried it.'

'Fibber!' said George at once.

'Now you listen to me,' began Alfredo again. 'If you fire-eat I will whip you till you beg me for mercy. I will . . .'

'Now, Fredo,' said his wife, 'you'll do nothing of the sort. I'll deal with Jo if she starts any nonsense here. As for fire-eating – well, if there's to be anyone else fire-eating here, *I* will do it, I, your wife.'

'You will *not* fire-eat,' said Alfredo obstinately, evidently afraid that his hot-tempered wife might try to do it.

Anne suddenly gave a scream of fright. A long, thick body glided between her and Julian – one of the snake-man's pythons! He had brought one with him, and the children hadn't known. Jo caught hold of it and held on for dear life.

'Let him be,' said the snake-man. 'He will come back to me. He wants a run.'

'Let me hold him for a bit,' begged Jo. 'He feels so smooth and cold. I like snakes.'

Julian put out his hand gingerly and touched the great snake. It did feel unexpectedly smooth, and quite cool. How extraordinary! It looked so scaly and rough.

The snake slithered all the way up Jo and then began to pour itself down her back. 'Now, don't you let him get his tail round you,' warned the snake-man. 'I've told you that before.'

'I'll wear him round my neck,' said Jo, and proceeded to pull the snake's long body until in the end he hung round her neck like a scarf. George watched in unwilling admiration. Anne had removed herself as far from Jo as possible. The boys gazed in astonishment, and felt a new respect for the little traveller girl.

Someone struck up a soft melody on a guitar. It was Skippy, Bufflo's wife. She hummed a sad little song that had a gay little chorus in which all the fair-folk joined. Practically all the camp had come along now, and there were quite a few the children hadn't seen before.

It was exciting sitting there round the glowing fire, listening to the thrum of the guitar, and the sound of Skippy's low, clear voice – sitting near a fire-eater too, and within arm's length of a snake who also seemed to be enjoying the music! He swayed about in time to the chorus, and then suddenly poured himself all down the front of Jo, and glided like magic to his master, the snake-man.

'Ah, my beauty,' said the funny little man, and let the python slide between his hands, its coils pulsing powerfully as it went. 'You like the music, my beauty?'

'He really loves his snake,' whispered Anne to George. 'How can he?'

Alfredo's wife got up. 'It is time to go,' she told the audience. 'Alfredo needs his supper. Is it not so, my big bad man?'

Alfredo agreed that it was so. He placed the heavy iron pot over the glowing fire again, and in a few seconds such a glorious smell came from it that all the five children began to sniff expectantly.

FIRE-EATING AND OTHER THINGS!

'Where's Timmy?' said George, suddenly. He was nowhere to be seen!

'He crept away with his tail down when he saw the snake,' said Jo. 'I saw him go. Timmy, come back! It's all right! Timmy, Timmy!'

'I'll call him, thank you,' said George. 'He's *my* dog. Timmy!'

Timmy came, his tail still down. George fondled him and so did Jo. He licked them both in turn. George tried to drag him away from Jo. She didn't like Timmy to show affection for the little traveller girl – but he always did! He loved her.

The supper was lovely. '*What* is in your pot?' asked Dick, accepting a second helping. 'I've never tasted such a delicious stew in my life.'

'Chicken, duck, beef, bacon, rabbit, hare, hedgehog, onions, turnips . . .' began Alfredo's wife. 'I put there everything that comes. It cooks and I stir, it cooks and I stir. Perhaps a partridge goes in one day, and a pheasant the next, and . . .'

'Hold your tongue, wife,' growled Alfredo, who knew quite well that the farmers round about might well ask questions about some of the things in that stew.

'You tell me to hold my tongue!' cried little Mrs Alfredo angrily, flourishing a spoon. 'You tell me that!'

'Woof,' said Timmy, receiving some nice tasty drops on his nose, and licking them off. 'Woof!' He got up and went towards the spoon, hoping for a few more.

'Oh, Aunt Nita, do give Timmy a spoonful out of the stew,' begged Jo, and to Timmy's great joy he got a big plateful all to himself. He could hardly believe it!

'Thank you very much for a very nice supper,' said Julian, feeling that it really was time to go. He got up and the others followed his example.

'And thank you for fire-eating for us, Alfredo,' said George. 'It doesn't seem to have spoilt your appetite!'

'Poof!' said Alfredo, as if such a thing would never enter his head. 'Jo – are you going to stay with us again tonight? You are welcome.'

'I'd just like an old rug, that's all, Aunt Nita,' said Jo. 'I'm going to sleep under George's caravan.'

'You can sleep on the floor inside, if you like,' said George. But Jo shook her head.

'No. I've had enough of sleeping indoors for a bit. I want to sleep out. Under the caravan will be a fine place for me. Travellers often sleep there when the weather is warm.'

They went back over the dark hillside. A few stars were out, but the moon was not yet up. 'That was a jolly interesting evening,' said Dick. 'I enjoyed it.

I like your aunt and uncle, Jo.'

Jo was delighted. She always loved praise from Dick. She went under the girls' caravan, and rolled herself up in the rug. She had been taught to clean her teeth and wash and do her hair but all that was forgotten now.

'In a day or two she'll be the dirty, tangly-haired, rude girl she was when we first knew her,' said George, combing out her own hair extra well. 'I'm glad we're going to stay here after all, aren't you, Anne? I really do think the fair people are friendly towards us now.'

'Thanks to Jo,' said Anne. George said nothing. She didn't like being under obligation to Jo! She finished preparing herself for bed and got into her bunk.

'I wish *we'd* seen that face at the window, don't you, Anne?' she said. 'I do wonder whose it was – and why it was there, looking out.'

'I don't think I want to talk about faces at windows just now,' said Anne, getting into her bunk. 'Let's change the subject.' She blew out the lamp and settled down. They talked for a few minutes, and then George heard something outside the caravan. What could it be? Timmy raised his head and gave a little growl.

George looked at the window opposite. A lone star shone through it – and then something came in front of the star, blotted it out, and pressed itself against the glass pane. Timmy growled again, but not very loudly. Was it someone he knew?'

George flashed on her torch, and immediately saw what it was. She gave a little giggle. Then she called to Anne.

'Anne! Anne! Quick, there's a face at the window. Anne, wake up!'

'I'm not asleep,' said Anne's voice, and she sat up, scared. 'What face? Where? You're not just frightening me, are you?'

'No – there it is, look!' said George and shone her torch at the window. A big, long, face looked in, and Anne gave a shriek. Then she laughed. 'You beast, George – it's only Alfredo's horse. Oh, you *did* give me a fright. I've a good mind to pull you out of your bunk on to the floor. Go away, you silly staring horse – shoo, go away!'

CHAPTER THIRTEEN

Off to the castle

NEXT MORNING, as they had breakfast, the children discussed the face at the castle window again. They had levelled the field-glasses time and again at the window, but there was nothing to be seen.

'Let's go and see over the castle as soon as it opens,' said Dick. 'But mind – nobody is to mention faces at windows – you hear me, Jo? You're the one who can't keep your tongue still sometimes.'

Jo flared up. 'I'm not! I can keep a secret!'

'All right, fire-eater,' said Dick with a grin. He looked at his watch. 'It's too soon to go yet.'

'I'll go and help Mr Slither with his snakes,' said Jo. 'Anyone else coming?'

'Mr Slither! What a marvellous name for a man who keeps snakes,' said Dick. 'I don't mind coming to watch, but I'm not keen on the way they pour themselves up and down people.'

They all went to Mr Slither's caravan except Anne, who said she would much rather clear up the breakfast things.

The snake-man had both his snakes out of their box. 'He *is* polishing them,' said George, sitting down nearby. 'See how he makes their brown bodies shine.'

'Here, Jo – you mop Beauty for me,' said Mr Slither. 'The stuff is in that bottle over there. He's got those nasty little mites again under his scales. Mop him with that stuff and that will soon get rid of them.'

Jo seemed to know what to do. She got a rag, tipped up the bottle of yellow stuff and began to pat one of the snakes gently, letting the lotion soak round his scales.

George, not to be outdone, offered to help in the polishing of the other snake. 'You hold him then,' said Mr Slither, and slid the snake over to George. He got up and went into his caravan. George hadn't quite bargained for this. The snake lay across her knees, and then began to wind round her body. 'Don't you let him get a hold of you with his tail,' Jo warned her.

The boys soon got tired of seeing Jo and George vying with one another over the pythons, and went off to where Bufflo was practising spinning rope rings. He spun loop after loop of rope, making wonderful patterns in the air with it. He grinned at the boys.

'Like a try?' he said. But neither of them could do anything with the rope at all.

'Let's see you snap off something with the whip-lash,' said Dick. 'I think you're a marvel at that.'

'What do you want me to hit?' asked Bufflo, picking up his magnificent whip. 'The topmost leaves on that bush?'

'Yes,' said Dick. Bufflo looked at them, swung his whip once or twice, lifted it – and cracked it.

Like magic the topmost leaves disappeared off the bush. The boys gazed in admiration. 'Now pick off that daisy-head over there,' said Julian, pointing.

Crack! The daisy-head vanished. 'That's easy,' said Bufflo. 'Look, you hold a pencil or something in your hand, one of you. I'll pick it out without touching your fingers!'

Julian hesitated. But Dick dived his hand into his pocket and brought out a red pencil, not very long. He held out his hand, with the pencil between finger and thumb. Bufflo looked at it with half-closed eyes, as if measuring the distance. He raised his whip.

Crack! The tip-end of the lash curled itself round the pencil and pulled it clean out of Dick's hand. It flew up into the air, and Bufflo reached out his hand and caught it!

'Jolly good,' said Dick, lost in admiration. 'Does it take long to learn a thing like that?'

'Matter of twenty years or so,' said Bufflo. 'But you want to begin when you're a nipper – about three years old, say. My pa taught me – and if I didn't learn fast enough he'd take the skin off the tips of my ears with his whip-lash! You soon learn if you know that's going to happen to you!'

The boys gazed at Bufflo's big ears. They certainly did look a bit rough at the edges!

'I throw knives too,' said Bufflo, basking in the boys' admiration. 'I put Skippy up against a board, and throw knives all round her – so that when she walks away from the board at the end, there's her shape all outlined in knives. Like to see me?'

'Well, no, not now,' said Julian, looking at his watch. 'We're going to see over the castle. Have you ever seen over it, Bufflo?'

'No. Who wants to waste time going over a ruined old castle?' said Bufflo, scornfully. 'Not me!'

He went off to his caravan, spinning rope rings as he went with an ease that Dick couldn't help envying from the bottom of his heart. What a pity he hadn't begun to learn these things early enough. He was afraid he would never be really good at them now. He was too old!

'George! Jo! It's time we went,' called Julian.

'Put down those snakes, and come along. Anne! Are you ready?'

Mr Slither went to collect his snakes. They glided over him in delight, and he ran his hands over their smooth, gleaming bodies.

'I must wash my hands before I go,' said George. 'They're a bit snaky. Coming, Jo?'

Jo didn't really see why it was necessary to wash snaky hands, but she went with George to the stream and they rinsed them thoroughly. George wiped her hands on a rather dirty hanky, and Jo wiped hers on a much dirtier skirt. She looked at George's jeans enviously. What a pity to have to wear skirts!

They didn't lock up the caravans. Julian felt sure that the fair-folk were now really friendly to them, and would not take anything from them themselves, nor permit anyone else to do so. They all walked down the hillside, Timmy bounding along joyfully, under the impression that he was going to take them for a nice long walk.

They climbed over the stile, walked up the lane a little way, and came to the wooden gate that opened on to the steep path up to the castle. Now that it was so near to them it looked almost as if it might fall on top of them!

They went up the path and came to the small tower in which was the little door giving entrance to the castle. An old woman was there, looking a little like a witch. If she had had green eyes Anne would most certainly have set her down as a descendant of a witch! But she had eyes like black beads. She had no teeth at all and it was difficult to understand what she said.

'Five, please,' said Julian, giving her twenty-five pence.

'You can't take the dog in,' said the old woman, mumbling so much that they couldn't make out what she said. She pointed to the dog and repeated her remark again, shaking her head all the time.

'Oh – can't we really take our dog?' said George. 'He won't do any harm.'

The old woman pointed to a set of rules: 'DOGS NOT ALLOWED IN.'

'All right. We'll leave him outside then,' said George, crossly. 'What a silly rule! Timmy, stay here. We won't be long.'

Timmy put his tail down. He didn't approve of this. But he knew that he was not allowed into certain places, such as churches, and he imagined this place must be an enormous church – the kind of place into which George so often disappeared on Sundays. He lay down in a sunny corner.

OFF TO THE CASTLE

The five children went in through the clicking turnstile. They opened the door beyond and went into the castle grounds. The door shut behind them.

'Wait – we ought to get a guidebook,' said Julian. 'I want to know something about that tower.'

He went back and bought one for another five pence. They stood in the great castle yard and looked at the book. It gave the history of the old place – a history of peace and war, quarrels and truces, family feuds, marriages and all the other things that make up history.

'It would be an exciting story if it was written up properly,' said Julian. 'Look – here's the plan. There *are* dungeons!'

'Not open to the public,' quoted Dick, in disappointment. 'What a pity.'

'It was once a very strong and powerful castle,' said Julian, looking at the plan. 'It always had the strong wall that is still round it – and the castle itself is built in the middle of a great courtyard that runs all round. It says the walls of the castle itself are eight feet thick. Eight feet thick! No wonder most of it is still standing!'

They looked at the silent ruins in awe. The castle towered up, broken here and there, with sometimes a whole wall missing, and with all the doorways misshapen.

'There were four towers, of course,' said Julian, still with his nose glued to the guidebook. 'It says three are almost completely ruined now – but the fourth one is in fairly good condition, though the stone stairway that led up to the top has fallen in.'

'Well then – you couldn't have seen a face at that window,' said George, looking up at the fourth tower. 'If the stairway has fallen in, no one could get up there.'

'Hm. We'll see how much fallen in it is,' said Julian. 'It may be dangerous to the public, and perhaps we'll find a notice warning us off – but it might be quite climbable in places.'

'Shall we go up it if so?' said Jo, her eyes shining. 'What shall we do if we find the face?'

'We'll wait till we find it first!' said Julian. He shut the guidebook and put it into his pocket. 'Well, we seem to be the only people here. Let's get going. We'll walk round the courtyard first.'

They walked round the courtyard that surrounded the castle. It was strewn with great white stones that had fallen from the walls of the castle itself. In one place a whole wall had fallen in, and they could see the inside of the castle, dark and forbidding.

They came round to the front of it again. 'Let's go in at the front door – if you can call that great stone archway that,' said Julian. 'I say – can't you imagine knights on horseback riding round this courtyard, impatient to be off to some tournament, their horses' hoofs clip-clopping all the time?'

'Yes!' said Dick. 'I can just imagine it!'

They went in at the arched entrance, and wandered through room after room with stone floors and walls, and with small slit-like windows that gave very little light indeed.

'They had no glass for panes in those days,' said Dick. 'I bet they were glad on cold windy days that the windows were so tiny. Brrrrrr! This must have been a terribly cold place to live in.'

'The floors used to be covered with rushes, and tapestry was hung on the walls,' said Anne, remembering a history lesson. 'Julian – let's go and look for the stairway to that tower now. Do let's! I'm longing to find out whether there really *is* a face up in that tower!'

CHAPTER FOURTEEN

Faynights Castle

'CHACK-CHACK-CHACK! Chack-chack-chack!' The jack-daws circled round the old castle, calling to one another in their cheerful, friendly voices. The five children looked up and watched them.

'You can see the grey at the backs of their necks,' said Dick. 'I wonder how many years jackdaws have lived round and about this castle.'

'I suppose the sticks lying all over this courtyard must have been dropped by them,' said Julian. 'They make their nests of big twigs – really, they must drop as many as they use! Just look at that pile over there!'

'Very wasteful of them!' said Dick. 'I wish they would come and drop some near our caravan to save me going to get firewood each day for the fire!'

They were standing at the great archway that made the entrance to the castle. Anne grew impatient. 'Do let's look at the towers now,' she said.

They went to the nearest one, but it was almost impossible to realise that it *had* been a tower. It was just a great heap of fallen stones, piled one on top of another.

They went to the only good tower. They had hoped to find some remains of a stone stairway, but to their great disappointment they could not even look up into the tower! One of the inner walls had fallen in, and the floor was piled up, completely blocked. There was no sign of a stairway. Either it too had fallen in, or it was covered by the stones of the ruined wall.

Julian was astonished. It was obvious that nobody could possibly climb up the tower from the inside! Then how in the world could there have been a face at the tower window? He began to feel rather uncomfortable. Was it a real face? If not, what could it have been?

'This is odd,' said Dick, thinking the same as Julian, and pointing to the heaped-up stones on the ground floor of the tower. 'It does look absolutely impossible for anyone to get up into the top of the tower. Well – what about that face then?'

'Let's go and ask that old woman if there *is* any way at all of getting up into the tower,' said Julian. 'She might know.'

So they left the castle, walked across the courtyard, back to the little tower in the outer wall that guarded the big gateway. The old woman was sitting by the turnstile, knitting.

'Could you tell us, please, if there is any way of getting up into the tower over there?' asked Julian

The old woman answered something, but it was difficult to understand a word she said. However, as she shook her head vigorously, it was plain that there *was* no way up to the tower. It was very puzzling.

'Is there a better plan of the castle than this?' asked Julian, showing his guidebook. 'A plan of the dungeons for instance – and a plan of the towers as they once were, before they were ruined?'

The old lady said something that sounded like 'Society of Reservation of something-or-other.'

'What did you say?' asked Julian, patiently.

The witch-like woman was evidently getting tired of these questions. She opened a big book that showed the amount of people and fees paid, and looked down it. She put her finger on something written there, and showed it to Julian.

'Society for Preservation of Old Buildings,' he read. 'Oh – did somebody come from them lately? Would they know more than it says in the guidebook?'

'Yes,' said the old woman. 'Two men came. They spent all day here – last Thursday. You ask that Society what you want to know – not me. I only take the money.'

She sounded quite intelligible all of a sudden. Then

she relapsed into mumbles again, and no one could understand a word.

'Anyway, she's told us what we want to know,' said Julian. 'We'll telephone the Society and ask them if they can tell us any more about the castle. There may be secret passages and things not shown in the guidebook at all.'

'How exciting!' said George, thrilled. 'I say, let's go back to that tower and look at the *outside* of it. It might be climbable there.'

They went back to see – but it *wasn't* climbable. Although the stones it was built of were uneven enough to form slight footholds and handholds it would be much too dangerous for anyone to try to climb up – even the cat-footed Jo. For one thing it would not be possible to tell which stones were loose and crumbling until the climber caught hold – and then down he would go!

All the same, Jo was willing to try. 'I might be able to do it,' she said, slipping off one of her shoes.

'Put your shoe on,' said Dick at once. 'You are NOT going to try any tricks of that sort. There isn't even ivy for you to cling to.'

Jo put back her shoe sulkily, looking astonishingly like George as she scowled. And then, to everyone's enormous astonishment, who should come bounding up to them but Timmy!

'Timmy! Wherever have you come from?' said George, in surprise. 'There's no way in except through the turnstile – and the door behind it is shut. We shut it ourselves! *How* did you get in?'

'Woof,' said Timmy, trying to explain. He ran to the good tower, made his way over the blocks of stone lying about and stopped by a small space between three or four of the fallen stones. 'Woof,' he said again, and pawed at one of the stones.

'He came out there,' said George. She tugged at a big stone, but she couldn't move it an inch, of course. 'I don't know how in the world Timmy squeezed himself out of this space – it doesn't look big enough for a rabbit. Certainly none of *us* could get inside!'

'What puzzles *me*,' said Julian, 'is how Timmy got in from the outside. We left him right outside the castle – so he must have run round the outer wall somewhere and found a small hole. He must have squeezed into that.'

'Yes. That's right,' said Dick. 'We know the walls are eight feet thick, so he must have found a place where a bit of it had broken at the bottom, and forced his way in. But – would there be a hole right through the whole thickness of eight feet?'

This was really puzzling. They all looked at Timmy, and he wagged his tail expectantly. Then he barked loudly and capered round as if he wanted a game.

The door behind the turnstile opened at once and the old lady appeared. 'How did that dog get here?' she called. 'He's to go out at once!'

'We don't know how he got in,' said Dick. 'Is there a hole in the outer wall?'

'No,' said the old woman. 'Not one. You must have let that dog in when I wasn't looking. He's to go out. And you too. You've been here long enough.'

'We may as well go,' said Julian. 'We've seen all there is to see – or all that we are *allowed* to see. I'm quite sure there is some way of getting up into that tower although the stairway is in ruins. I'm going to ring up the Society for the Preservation of Old Buildings and ask them to put me in touch with the fellows who examined the castle last week. They must have been experts.'

'Yes. They would probably have a complete plan,' said Dick. 'Secret passages, dungeons, hidden rooms and all – if there are any!'

They took Timmy by the collar, and went out through the turnstiles, click-click-click. 'I feel like having a couple of doughnuts at the dairy,' said George. 'And some lemonade. Anyone else feel the same?'

Everyone did, including Timmy, who barked at once.

'Timmy's silly over those doughnuts,' said George. 'He just wolfs them down.'

'It's a great waste,' said Anne. 'He ate four last time – more than anyone else had.'

They walked down to the village. 'You go and order what we want,' said Julian, 'and I'll just go and look up this Society. It may have an office somewhere in this district.'

He went to the post office to use the telephone there, and the rest of them trooped in at the door of the bright little dairy. The plump shop-woman welcomed them beamingly. She considered them her best customers, and they certainly were.

They were each on their second doughnut when Julian came back. 'Any news?' asked Dick.

'Yes,' said Julian. 'Peculiar news, though. I found the address of the Society – they've got a branch about fifty miles from here – that deals with all the old buildings for a radius of a hundred miles. I asked if they had any recent booklet about the castle.'

He stopped to take a doughnut, and bit into it. The others waited patiently while he chewed.

'They said they hadn't. The last time they had checked

over Faynights Castle was two years ago.'

'But – but what about those two men who came from the Society last week, then?' said George.

'Yes. That's what *I* said,' answered Julian, taking another bite. 'And here's the peculiar bit. They said they didn't know what I was talking about, nobody had been sent there from the Society, and who was I, anyhow?'

'Hmm!' said Dick, thinking hard. 'Then – those men were examining and exploring the castle for their own reasons!'

'I agree,' said Julian. 'And I can't help thinking that the face at the window and those two men have something to do with one another. It's quite clear that the men had nothing whatever to do with any official society – they merely gave it as an excuse because they wanted to find out what kind of hiding-place the castle had.'

The others stared at him, feeling a familiar excitement rising in them – what George called the 'adventure feeling'.

'Then there *was* a real face at that tower window, and there *is* a way of getting up there,' said Anne.

'Yes,' said Julian. 'I know it sounds very far-fetched, but I do think there is just a possibility that those two scientists have gone there. I don't know if you read it in the paper, but one of them, Jeffrey Pottersham, has written a book on famous ruins. He would know all about Faynights Castle, because it's a very well-known one. If they wanted to hide somewhere till the hue and cry had died down, and then escape to another country, well . . .'

'They could hide in the tower, and then quietly slip out from the castle one night, go down to the sea, and hire a fishing boat!' cried Dick, taking the words out of Julian's mouth. 'They'd be across the Channel in no time.'

'Yes. That's what I'd worked out too,' said Julian. 'I rather think I'll telephone Uncle Quentin about this. I'll describe the face as well as I can to him. I feel this is all rather too important to manage quite on our own. Those men may have extremely important secrets.'

'It's an adventure again,' said Jo, her face serious, but her eyes very bright. 'Oh – I'm *glad* I'm in it too!'

CHAPTER FIFTEEN

An interesting day

EVERYONE BEGAN to feel distinctly excited. 'I think I'll catch the bus into the next town,' said Julian. 'The telephone-box here is too easily overheard. I'd rather go to a kiosk somewhere in a street, where nobody can hear what I'm saying.'

'All right. You go,' said Dick. 'We'll do some shopping and go back to the caravans. I wonder what Uncle Quentin will say!'

Julian went off to the bus stop. The others wandered in and out of the few village shops, doing their shopping. Tomatoes, lettuces, mustard and cress, sausage rolls, fruit cake, tins of fruit, and plenty of creamy milk in big quart bottles.

They met some of the fair-folk in the street, and everyone was very friendly indeed. Mrs Alfredo was there with an enormous basket, nearly as big as herself. She beamed and called across to them.

'You see I have to do my shopping myself! That big bad man is too lazy to do it for me. And he has no brains. I tell him to bring back meat and he brings fish, I tell him to buy cabbage and he brings lettuce. He has no brains!'

The children laughed. It was strange to find great big Alfredo, a real fire-eater, ordered about and grumbled at by his tiny wife.

'It's a change to find them all so friendly,' said George, pleased. 'Long may it last. There's the snake-man, Mr Slither – he hasn't got his snakes with him, though.'

'He'd have the whole village to himself if he did!' said Anne. 'I wonder what he buys to feed his snakes on.'

'They're only fed once a fortnight,' said Jo. 'They swallow . . .'

'No, don't tell me,' said Anne, hastily. 'I don't really want to know. Look, there's Skippy.'

Skippy waved cheerily. She carried bags filled to bursting too. The fair-folk certainly did themselves well.

'They must make a lot of money,' said Anne.

'Well, they spend it when they have it,' said Jo. 'They never save. It's either a good time for them or a very bad time. They must have had a good run at the last show-place – they all seem very rich!'

AN INTERESTING DAY

They went back to the camp and spent a very interesting day, because the fair-folk, eager to make up for their unfriendly behaviour, made them all very welcome. Alfredo explained his fire-eating a little more, and showed how he put wads of cotton wool at the hook-end of his torches, and then soaked them in petrol to flare easily.

The rubber-man obligingly wriggled in and out of the wheel-spokes of his caravan, a most amazing feat. He also doubled himself up, and twisted his arms and legs together in such a peculiar manner that he seemed to be more like a four-tentacled octopus than a human being.

He offered to teach Dick how to do this, but Dick couldn't even bend himself properly double. He was disappointed because he couldn't help thinking what a marvellous trick it would be to perform in the playing field at school.

Mr Slither gave them a most entertaining talk about snakes, and ended up with some information about poisonous snakes that he said they might find very useful indeed.

'Take rattlers now,' he said, 'or mambas, or any poisonous snake. If you want to catch one to tame, don't go after it with a stick, or pin it to the ground.

That frightens it and you can't do anything with it.'

'What do you have to do then?' asked George.

'Well, you want to watch their forked tongues,' said Mr Slither, earnestly. 'You know how they put them out, and make them quiver and shake?'

'Yes,' said everyone.

'Well, now, if a poisonous snake makes its tongue go all stiff without a quiver in it, just be careful,' said Mr Slither, solemnly. 'Don't you touch it then. But if its tongue is nice and quivery, just slide your arms along its body, and it will let you pick it up.' He went through the motions he described, picking up a pretend snake and letting its body slither through his arms. It was fascinating to watch, but very weird.

'Thanks most awfully,' said Dick. 'Whenever I pick up poisonous snakes, I'll do exactly as you say.'

The others laughed. Dick sounded as if he went about picking up poisonous snakes every day! Mr Slither was pleased to have such an appreciative audience. George and Anne, however, had firmly made up their minds that they were not going even to *look* at a snake's tongue if it put it out – they were going to run for miles!

There were a few more fair-folk there that the children didn't know much about – Dacca, the tap-dancer, who put on high boots and tap-danced for the children on the top step of her caravan – Pearl, who was an acrobat and could walk on wire-rope, dance on it, and turn somersaults over it, landing back safely each time – and others who belonged to the show but only helped with the crowds and the various turns.

Jo didn't know them all, but she was soon so much one of them that the children began to wonder if she would ever go back to her foster-mother again!

'She's exactly like them all now,' said George. 'Cheerful, slapdash and generous, lazy and yet hardworking too! Bufflo practises for hours at his rope-spinning, but he lies about for hours too. They're strange folk, but I really do like them very much.'

The others agreed with her heartily. They had their lunch without Julian, because he hadn't come back. Why was he so long? He only had to telephone his uncle!

He came back at last. 'Sorry I'm so late,' he said, 'but first of all I couldn't get any answer at all, so I waited a bit in case Aunt Fanny and Uncle Quentin were out – and I had lunch while I waited. Then I telephoned again, and Aunt Fanny was in, but Uncle Quentin had gone to London and wouldn't be back till night.'

'To London!' said George, astonished. 'He hardly ever goes to London.'

'Apparently he went up about these two missing scientists,' said Julian. 'He's so certain that his friend Terry-Kane isn't a traitor, and he went up to tell the authorities so. Well, I couldn't wait till night, of course.'

'Didn't you report our news then?' said Dick, disappointed.

'Yes. But I had to tell Aunt Fanny,' said Julian. 'She said she would repeat it all to Uncle Quentin when he came back tonight. It's a pity I couldn't get hold of him and find out what he thinks. I asked Aunt Fanny to tell him to write to me at once.'

After tea they sat on the hillside again, basking in the sun. It really was wonderful weather for them. Julian looked over to the ruined castle opposite. He fixed his eyes on the tower where they had seen the face. It was so far away that he could only just make out the window-slit.

'Get your glasses, George,' he said. 'We may as well have another squint at the window. It was about this time that we saw the face.'

George fetched them. She would not give them to Julian first though – she put them to her own eyes and gazed at the window. At first she saw nothing – and then, quite suddenly, a face appeared at the window! George was so astonished that she cried out.

AN INTERESTING DAY

Julian snatched the glasses from her. He focused them on the window and saw the face at once. Yes – the same as yesterday – eyebrows and all!

Dick took the glasses, and then each of them in turn gazed at the strange face. It did not move at all, as far as they could see, but simply stared. Then, when Anne was looking at it, it suddenly disappeared and did not come back again.

'Well – we *didn't* imagine it yesterday then,' said Julian. 'It's there all right. And where there's a face, there should be a body. Er – did any of you think that the face had a – a sort of – despairing expression?'

'Yes,' said Dick and the others agreed. 'I thought so yesterday, too,' said Dick. 'Do you suppose the fellow, whoever he is, is being kept prisoner up there?'

'It looks like it,' said Julian. 'But how in the world did he get there? It's a marvellous place to put him, of course. Nobody would ever dream of a hiding-place like that – and if it hadn't been for us looking at the jackdaws through very fine field-glasses, we'd never have seen him looking out. It was a chance in a thousand that we saw him.'

'In a *million*,' said Dick. 'Look here, Ju – I think we ought to go up to the castle and yell up to the fellow – he might be able to yell back, or throw a message out.'

'He would have thrown out a message before now if he'd been able to,' said Julian. 'As for yelling, he'd have to lean right out of that thick-walled window to make himself heard. He's right at the back of it, remember, and the slit is very deep.'

'Can't we go and find out something?' said George, who was longing to take some action. 'After all, Timmy got in somewhere, and we might be able to as well.'

'That's quite an idea,' said Julian. 'Timmy *did* find a way in – and it may be the way that leads up to the top of the tower.'

'Let's go then,' said George at once.

'Not now,' said Julian. 'We'd be seen if we scrambled about on the hill outside the castle walls. We'd have to go at night. We could go when the moon comes up.'

A shiver of excitement ran through the whole five. Timmy thumped his tail on the ground. He had been listening all the time, just as if he understood.

'We'll take you too, Timmy,' said George, 'just in case we run into any trouble.'

'We shan't get into trouble,' said Julian. 'We're only going to explore – and I don't think for a minute we'll find much, because I'm sure we shan't be able to get up into the tower. But I expect you all feel like I do – you can't leave this mystery of the face at the window alone

– you want to *do* something about it, even if it's only scrambling round the old walls at night.'

'Yes. That's *exactly* how I feel,' said George. 'I wouldn't be able to go to sleep tonight, I know. Oh, Julian – isn't this exciting?'

'Very,' said Julian. 'I'm glad we didn't leave today, after all! We should have, if we hadn't seen that face at the window.'

The sun went down and the air grew rather cold. They went into the boys' caravan and played cards, not feeling at all sleepy. Jo was very bad at cards, and soon stopped playing. She sat watching, her arm round Timmy's neck.

They had a supper of sausage rolls and tinned strawberries. 'It's a pity they don't have meals like this at school,' said Dick. 'No trouble to prepare, and most delicious to eat. Julian – is it time to go?'

'Yes,' said Julian. 'Put on warm things – and we'll set off! Here's to a really adventurous night!'

CHAPTER SIXTEEN

Secret ways

THEY WAITED till the moon went behind a cloud, and then, like moving shadows, made their way down the hillside as fast as they could. They did not want any of the fair-folk to see them. They clambered over the stile and went up the lane. They made their way up the steep path to the castle, but when they came to the little tower where the turnstile was they went off to the right, and walked round the foot of the great, thick walls.

It was difficult to walk there, because the slope of the hill was so steep. Timmy went with them, excited at this unexpected walk.

'Now, Timmy, listen – we want you to show us how you got in,' said George. 'Are you listening, Timmy? Go in, Timmy, go in where you went this morning.'

Timmy waved his long tail, panted, and let his tongue hang out in the way he did when he wanted to show he was being as helpful as he could. He ran in front, sniffing.

Then he suddenly stopped and looked back. He gave a little whine. The others hurried to him.

The moon most annoyingly went behind a cloud. Julian took out his torch and shone it where Timmy stood. The dog stood there, looking very pleased.

'Well, what is there to be pleased about, Timmy?' said Julian, puzzled. 'There's no hole there – nowhere you could possibly have got in. What are you trying to show us?'

Timmy gave a little bark. Then suddenly leapt about four feet up the uneven stones of the wall, and disappeared!

'Hey – where's he gone?' said Julian, startled. He flashed his torch up. 'I say, look! There's a stone missing up there, quite a big block – and Timmy's gone in at the hole.'

'There's the block – fallen down the hillside,' said Dick, pointing to a big white stone, roughly square in shape. 'But how has Timmy gone in, Ju? This wall is frightfully thick, and even if one stone falls out, there must be plenty more behind!'

Julian climbed up. He came to the space where the great fallen stone had been and flashed his torch there. 'I say – this is interesting!' he called. 'The wall is hollow just here. Timmy's gone into the hollow!'

At once a surge of excitement went through the whole lot. 'Can we get in and follow Timmy?' called George.

'Shout to him, Julian, and see where he is.'

Julian called into the hollow. 'Timmy! Timmy, where are you?'

A distant, rather muffled bark answered him, and then Timmy's eyes suddenly gleamed up at Julian. The dog was standing down in the small hollow behind the fallen stone. 'He's here,' called back Julian. 'I tell you what I think we've hit on. When this enormous wall was built, a space was left inside – either to save stones, or to make a hidden passage, I don't know which. And that fallen stone has exposed a bit of the hollow. Shall we explore?'

'Oh, *yes*,' came the answer at once. Julian climbed down into the middle of the wall. He flashed his torch into the space he was standing in. 'Yes,' he called, 'it's a kind of passage. It's small, though. We'll have to bend almost double to get along it. Anne, you come next, then I can help you.'

'Will the air be all right?' called Dick into the passage.

'It smells a bit musty,' said Julian. 'But if it really *is* a passage, there must be secret air-holes somewhere to keep the air fresh in here. That's right, Anne – you hang on to me. Jo, you come next, then George, then Dick.'

Soon they were all in the curious passage, which ran along in the centre of the wall. It certainly was very small. They all got tired of going along bent double. It was pitch dark too, and although they all had torches, except Jo, it was very difficult to see.

Anne hung on to Julian's jacket for dear life. She wasn't enjoying this very much, but she wouldn't have been left out of it for anything.

Julian suddenly stopped, and everyone bumped into the one in front. 'What's up?' called Dick, from the back.

'Steps here!' shouted back Julian. 'Steps going down very, very steeply – almost like a stone ladder. Be careful, everybody!'

The steps were certainly steep. 'Better go down backwards,' decided Julian. 'Then we can have handholds as well as footholds. Anne, wait till I'm down and I'll help you.'

The steps went down for about ten feet. Julian got down safely, then Anne turned herself round and went down backwards too, as if she were on a ladder instead of on stairs. It was much easier that way.

At the bottom was another passage, wider and higher, for which everyone was devoutly thankful. 'Where does *this* lead to?' said Julian, stopping to think. 'This passage is at right angles to the wall – we've left the wall now – we're going underneath part of the courtyard, I should think.'

'I bet we're not far from that tower,' called Dick. 'I say – I do hope this leads to the tower.'

Nobody could possibly tell where it was going to lead to! Anyway, it seemed to run quite straight, and after about eighty feet of it, Julian stopped again.

'Steps up again!' he called. 'Just as steep as the others. I think we may be going up into the inside of the castle walls. This is possibly a secret way into one of the old rooms of the castle.'

They went carefully up the steep stone steps and found themselves, not in a passage, but in a very small room that appeared to be hollowed out of the wall of the castle itself. Julian stopped in surprise, and everyone crowded into the tiny room. It really wasn't much larger than a big cupboard. A narrow bench stood at one side, with a shelf above it. An old pitcher stood on the shelf, with a broken lip, and on the bench was a small dagger, rusty and broken.

'I say! Look here! This is a secret room – like they used to have in old places, so that someone might hide if necessary,' said Julian. 'We're inside one of the walls of the castle itself – perhaps the wall of an old bedroom!'

'And there's the old pitcher that had water in,' said George. 'And a dagger. Who hid here – and how long ago?'

Dick flashed his torch round to see if he could anything else. He gave a sudden exclamation, and k his torch fixed on a corner of the room.

'What is it?' said Julian.

'Paper – red and blue silver paper,' said Dick. 'Chocolate wrapping! How many times have we bought this kind of chocolate, wrapped in silver paper patterned with red and blue!'

He picked it up and straightened it out. Yes – there was the name of the chocolate firm on it!

Everyone was silent. This could only mean one thing. *Someone* had been in this room lately – someone who ate chocolate – someone who had thrown down the wrapping never expecting it to be found!

'Well,' said Julian, breaking the silence. 'This *is* surprising. Someone else knows this way in. Where does it lead to? Up to that tower, I imagine!'

'Hadn't we better be careful?' said Dick, lowering his voice. 'I mean – whoever was here might quite well be wandering about somewhere near.'

'Yes. Perhaps we'd better go back,' said Julian, thinking of the girls.

'No,' said George, in a fierce whisper. 'Let's go on. We can be very cautious.'

A passage led from the strange hidden room. It went

ttle way, and then they arrived

ran straight upwards like

...e to a small, very narrow door. It

, old-fashioned iron ring for a handle.

Julian stood hesitating. Should he open it or not? He stood for half a minute, trying to make up his mind. He whispered back to the others. 'I've come to a little door. Shall I open it?'

'Yes,' came back the answering whispers. Julian cautiously took hold of the iron ring. He turned it, and it made no noise. He wondered if the door was locked on the other side. But it wasn't. It opened silently.

Julian looked through it, expecting to see a room, but there wasn't one. Instead he found himself on a small gallery that seemed to run all the way round the inside of the tower. The moon shone in through a slit-window, and Julian could just make out that he must be looking down from a gallery into the darkness of a tower room on the second or third floor of the tower – the third, probably.

He pulled Anne out and the other three followed. There was no sound to be heard. Julian whispered to the others. 'We've come out on to a gallery, which overlooks one of the rooms inside the tower. It may be a second-floor room, because we know that the ceiling of the first floor has fallen in. Or perhaps it's even the third floor.'

'Must be the third,' said Dick. 'We're pretty high.' His whisper went all round the gallery and came back to them. He had spoken more loudly than Julian. It made them jump.

'How do we get higher still?' whispered George.

'Is there any way up from this gallery?'

'We'll walk round it and see,' said Julian. 'Be as quiet as you can. I don't *think* there's anyone here, but you never know. And watch your step, in case the stone isn't sound – it's very crumbly here and there.'

Julian led the way round the curious little gallery. Had this tower room been used for old plays or mimes? Was the gallery for spectators? He wished he could turn back the years and lean over the gallery to see what had been going on in the room below, when the castle was full of people.

About three-quarters of the way round the gallery a little flight of steps led downwards into the room below. But just beyond where the steps began there was another door set in the wall, very like the one they had just come through.

It too had an iron ring for a handle. Julian turned it slowly. It didn't open. Was it locked? There was a great key standing in the iron lock, and Julian turned it. But still the door didn't open. Then he saw that it was bolted.

The bolt was securely pushed home. So somebody was a prisoner on the other side! Was it the man who owned the Face? Julian turned and whispered very softly in Anne's ear.

'There's a door here bolted on my side. Looks as if we're coming to the Face. Tell George to send Timmy right up to me.'

Anne whispered to George, and George pushed Timmy forward. He squeezed past Anne's legs and stood by Julian, sensing the sudden excitement.

'We're probably coming to stairs that lead up to the top tower room, where that window is with the face,' thought Julian, as he slid back the bolt very cautiously. He pushed the door, and it opened. He stood listening, his torch switched off. Then he switched it on.

Just as he had thought, another stone stairway led up steeply. At the top must be the prisoner, whoever he was.

'We'll go up,' said Julian softly. 'Quiet, everybody!'

CHAPTER SEVENTEEN

Excitement and shocks

TIMMY STRAINED forward, but Julian had his hand on the dog's collar. He went up the stone stairway, very steep and narrow. The others followed with hardly a sound. All of them but Jo had on their rubber shoes; she had bare feet. Timmy made the most noise, because his claws clicked on the stone.

At the top was another door. From behind it came a curious noise – guttural and growling. Timmy growled in his throat. At first Julian couldn't think what the noise was. Then he suddenly knew.

'Somebody snoring! Well, that's lucky. I can take a peep in and see who it is. We must be at the top of the tower now.'

The door in front of him was not locked. He pushed it open and looked inside, his hand still on Timmy's collar.

The moonlight struck through a narrow window and fell on the face of a sleeping man. Julian stared at it in rising excitement. Those eyebrows! Yes – this was the man whose face had appeared at the window!

'And I know who he is too – it *is* Terry-Kane!' thought Julian, moving like a shadow into the room. 'He's exactly like the picture we saw in the papers. Perhaps the other man is here too.'

He looked cautiously round the room but could see no one else, although it was possible there might be someone in the darkest shadows. He listened.

There was only the snoring of the man lying in the moonlight. He could not hear the breathing of anyone else. With his hand still on Timmy's collar he switched on his torch and swept it round the tower room, its beam piercing the black corners.

No one was there except the one man – and, with a sudden shock, Julian saw that he was tied with ropes! His arms were bound behind him and his legs were tied together too. If this was Terry-Kane then his uncle must be right. The man was no traitor – he had been kidnapped and was a prisoner.

Everyone was now in the room, staring at the sleeping man. He had his mouth open, and he still snored loudly.

'What are you going to do, Julian?' whispered George. 'Wake him up?'

Julian nodded. He went over to the sleeping man and

shook him by the shoulder. He woke up at once and stared in amazement at Julian, who was full in the moonlight. He struggled up to a sitting position.

'Who are you?' he said. 'How did you get here – and who are those over in the shadows there?'

'Listen – are you Mr Terry-Kane?' asked Julian.

'Yes. I am. But who are you?'

'We are staying on the hill opposite the castle,' said Julian. 'And we saw your face at the window, through our field-glasses. So we came to find you.'

'But – but how do you know who I am?' said the man, still amazed.

'We read about you in the papers,' said Julian. 'And we saw your picture. We couldn't help noticing your eyebrows, sir – we even saw them through the glasses.'

'Look here – can you undo me?' said the man, eagerly. 'I must escape. Tomorrow night my enemies are smuggling me out of here, into a car and down to the sea – and a boat is being hired to take me across to the Continent. They want me to tell them what I know about my latest experiments. I shan't, of course – but life wouldn't be at all pleasant for me!'

'I'll cut the ropes,' said Julian, and he took out his pocket-knife. He cut the knots that tied Terry-Kane's wrists together and then freed his legs. Timmy stood and watched, ready to pounce if the man did anything fierce!

'That's better,' said the man, stretching his arms out.

'How did you manage to get to the window?' asked Julian, watching the man rub his arms and knees.

'Each evening one of the men who brought me here comes to bring me food and drink,' said Terry-Kane. 'He undoes my hands so that I can feed myself. He sits and smokes while I eat, taking no notice of me. I drag myself over to the window to have a breath of fresh air. I can't stay there long because I am soon tied up again, of course. I can't imagine how anyone could see my face at this deep-set slit-window!'

'It was our field-glasses,' said Julian. 'They are such fine ones. It's a good thing you *did* get to the window for a breath of air or we'd never have found you!'

'Julian – I can hear a noise,' said Jo, suddenly. She had ears like a cat, able to pick up the slightest sound.

'Where?' said Julian, turning sharply.

'Downstairs,' whispered Jo. 'Wait – I'll go and see.'

She slipped out of the door and down the steep little stairs. She came to the door at the bottom, the one that led into the gallery.

Yes – someone was coming! Coming along the gallery

too. Jo thought quickly. If she darted back up the stairs to warn the others, this newcomer might go up there too, and they would all be caught. He could bolt the door at the top and would have six prisoners instead of one! She decided to crouch down on the floor of the gallery a little beyond the door that led upwards.

Footsteps came loudly along the gallery and up to the door. Then the stranger obviously found the door unbolted, and stopped in consternation. He stood perfectly still, listening. Jo thought he really must be able to hear her heart beating, it was thumping so loudly. She didn't dare to call out to try and warn the others – if she did they would walk straight into his arms!

And then Jo heard Julian's voice calling quietly down the stone stairs. 'Jo! Jo! Where are you?' And then, oh dear, she thought she could hear Julian coming down the stairs to find her. 'Don't come, Julian,' she said under her breath. 'Don't come.'

But Julian came right down – and behind him came Terry-Kane and Dick, with the girls following with Timmy, on their way to escaping.

The stranger down at the door was even more amazed to hear voices and footsteps. He slammed the door suddenly and rammed the stout bolt home. The footsteps on the stairs stopped in alarm.

'Hey, Jo! Is that you?' called Julian's voice. 'Open the door!'

The stranger spoke angrily. 'The door's bolted. Who are you?'

There was a silence – then Terry-Kane answered. 'So you're back again, Pottersham! Open that door at once.'

'Oho!' thought Julian. 'So the other scientist is here too – Jeffrey Pottersham. He must have got Terry-Kane here by kidnapping him. What can have happened to Jo?'

The man at the door stood there as if he didn't quite know what to do. Jo crouched down in the gallery and listened intently. The man spoke again.

'Who set you free? Who's that with you?'

'Now, listen, Pottersham,' said Terry-Kane's voice. 'I've had enough of this nonsense. You must be out of your mind, acting like this! Doping me, and kidnapping me, telling me we're going to go off by fishing boat to the Continent, and the rest of it! There are four children here, who saw my face at the window and came to investigate, and . . .'

'*Children!*' said Pottersham, taken aback. 'What, in the middle of the night! How did they get up to this tower? I'm the only one that knows the way in.'

EXCITEMENT AND SHOCKS

'Pottersham, open the door!' shouted Terry-Kane, furiously. He gave it a kick, but the old door was sturdy and strong.

'You can go back to the tower, all of you,' said Pottersham. 'I'm going off to get fresh orders. It looks as if we'll have to take those kids with us, Terry-Kane – they'll be sorry they saw your face at the window. They won't like life where we're going!'

Pottersham turned and went back the way he had come. Jo guessed that he knew the same way in as they had happened on. She waited until she felt that it was perfectly safe, and then she ran to the door again. She hammered on it.

'Dick! Dick! Come down. Where are you?' She heard an answering shout from up the stairs behind the door, and then Dick came running down.

'Jo! Unbolt the door, quick!'

Jo unbolted it – but it wouldn't open. Julian had now come down too, and he called to Jo: 'Turn the key, Jo. It may be locked too.'

'Julian, the key's gone!' cried Jo, and she tugged in vain at the door. 'He must have locked it as well as bolted it – and he's taken the key. Oh, how can I get you out?'

'You can't,' said Dick. 'Still, *you're* free, Jo. You can go and tell the police. Buck up, now. You know the way, don't you?'

'I haven't got a torch,' said Jo.

'Oh dear – well, we can't possibly get one of ours out to you,' said Dick. 'You'd better wait till morning, then, Jo. You may lose yourself down in those dark passages. Yes – wait till morning.'

'The passages will still be dark!' said poor Jo. 'I'd better go now.'

'No – you're to wait till morning,' said Julian, fearing that Jo might wander off in the strange passages, and be lost for ever! She might even find herself down in the dungeons. Horrible thought.

'All right,' said Jo. 'I'll wait till morning. I'll curl up on the gallery here. It's quite warm.'

'It will be very hard!' said Dick. 'We'll go back to the room upstairs, Jo. Call us if you want us. What a blessing you're free!'

Jo curled up on the gallery, but she couldn't sleep. For one thing the floor was very hard, and the stone was very, very cold. She suddenly thought of the little room where they had seen the pitcher, the dagger and the chocolate wrapping paper. That would be a far better place to sleep! She could lie on the bench!

She stood up and thought out the way. All she had to

do was to go round the gallery till she came to the little
door that opened on to the corkscrew staircase leading
from the gallery to the little hidden room.

She made her way cautiously to the door. She felt for
the iron ring, turned it and opened the door. It was very,
very dark, and she could see nothing at all in front of
her. She put out her foot carefully. Was she at the top
of the spiral staircase?

She found that she was. She held out her hands on
either side, touching the stone walls of the curious little
stairway, and went slowly down, step by step.

'Oh dear – am I going the right way? The stairs seem
to be going on so long!' thought Jo. 'I don't like it – but
I MUST go on!'

CHAPTER EIGHTEEN

Jo has an adventure on her own

JO CAME to the end of the spiral stairway at last. She found herself on the level once more, and remembered the little straight passage that led to the secret room from the stairway. Good, good, good! Now she would soon be in the room and could lie down on the bench.

She went through the doorway of the secret room without knowing it, because it was so dark. She groped her way along, and suddenly felt the edge of the bench.

'Here at last,' she said thankfully, out loud.

And then poor Jo got a dreadful shock! A pair of strong arms went round her and held her fast! She screamed and struggled, her heart beating in wild alarm. Who was it? Oh, if only she had a light!

And then a torch was switched on, and held to her face. 'Oho! You must be Jo, I suppose,' said Pottersham's voice. 'I wondered who you were when one of those kids yelled out for you! I thought you must be wandering somewhere about. I guessed you'd come this way, and I sat on the bench and waited for you.'

JO HAS AN ADVENTURE ON HER OWN

'Let me go,' said Jo fiercely and struggled like a wild cat. The man only held her all the more tightly. He was very strong.

Jo suddenly put down her face and bit his hand. He gave a shout and loosened his hold. Jo was almost free when he caught her again, and shook her like a rat. 'You little wild cat! Don't you do that again!'

Jo did it again, even more fiercely, and the man dropped her on to the ground, nursing his hand. Jo made for the entrance of the room, but again the man was too quick and she found herself held again.

'I'll tie you up,' said the man, furiously. 'I'll rope you so that you won't be able to move! And I'll leave you here in the dark till I come back again.'

He took a rope from round his waist and proceeded to tie Jo up so thoroughly that she could hardly move. Her hands were behind her back, her legs were tied at the knees and ankles. She rolled about the floor, calling the man all the names she knew.

'Well, you're safe for the time being,' said Pottersham, sucking his bitten hand. 'Now I'm going. I wish you joy of the hard, cold floor and the darkness, you little wild cat!'

Jo heard his footsteps going in the distance. She could have kicked herself for not having guessed he might have been lying in wait for her. Now she couldn't get help for the others. In fact, she was much worse off than they were because she was tied up, and they weren't.

Poor Jo! She dozed off, exhausted by the night's excitement and her fierce struggle. She lay against the wall, so uncomfortable that she kept waking from her doze every few minutes.

And then a thought came into her head. She remembered the rope-man, all tied up in length after length of knotted rope. She had watched him set himself free so many times. Could any of his tricks help her now?

'The rope-man would be able to get himself free of this rope in two minutes!' she thought, and began to wriggle and struggle again. But she was not the rope-man, and after about an hour she was so exhausted again that she went into a doze once more.

When she awoke, she felt better. She forced herself into a sitting position, and made herself think clearly and slowly.

'Work one knot free first,' she said to herself, remembering what the rope-man had told her. 'At first you won't know which knot is best. When you know that you will always be able to free yourself in two minutes. But find that one knot first!'

She said all this to herself as she tried to find a knot that might be worked loose. At last one seemed a little looser than the others. It was one that bound her left wrist to her right. She twisted her wrist round and got her thumb to the knot. She picked and pulled and at last it loosened a little. She had more control over that hand now. If only she had a knife somewhere! She could manage to get it between her finger and thumb now and perhaps use it to cut another knot.

She suddenly lost her patience and flung her head back on the bench, straining and pulling at the rope. She knocked against something and it fell to the stone floor with a clatter. Jo wondered what it was – and then she knew.

'That dagger! The old, rusty dagger! Oh, if I could find it I might do something with it!'

She swung herself round on the floor till she felt the dagger under her. She rolled over on her back and tried to pick it up with her free finger and thumb, and at last she managed to hold it.

She sat up, bent forward and did her best to force the rusty dagger up and down a little on the rope that tied her hands behind her. She could hardly move it at all because her hands were still so tightly tied. But she persevered.

She grew so tired that she had to give it up for a long while. Then she tried again, then had another long rest. The third time she was lucky! The rope suddenly frayed and broke! She pulled her hands hard, found them looser and picked at a knot.

It took Jo a long time to free her hands, but she did it at last. She couldn't manage to undo her legs at first, because her hands were trembling so much. But after another long rest she undid the tight knots, and shook her legs free. 'Well, thank goodness I learnt a few hints from the rope-man,' she said, out loud. 'I'd never have got free if I hadn't!'

She wondered what the time was. It was pitch dark in the little room, of course. She stood up and was surprised to find that her legs were shaky. She staggered a few steps and then sat down again. But her legs soon felt better and she stood up once more. 'Now to find my way out,' she said. 'How I wish I had a torch!'

She went carefully down the flight of stone steps that led down from the room, and then came to the wide passage that ran under the courtyard. She went along it, glad it was level, and then came once again to stone steps that led upwards. Up she climbed, knowing that she was going the right way, although she was in the dark.

Now she came to the small passage where she had to

bend almost double, the one that ran through the centre of the thick outer walls. Jo heaved a sigh of relief. Surely she would soon come to where the stone had fallen out and would be able to see daylight!

She saw daylight before she came to the place where the stone was missing. She saw it some way in front of her, a misty little patch that made her wonder what it was at first. Then she knew.

'Daylight! Oh, thank goodness!' She stumbled along to it and climbed up to the hole from which the stone had fallen. She sat there, drinking in the sunlight. It was bright and warm and very comforting.

After the darkness of the passages Jo felt quite dazed. Then she suddenly realised how very high the sun was in the sky! Goodness, it must be afternoon!

She looked cautiously out of the hole in the wall. Now that she was so near freedom she didn't want to be caught by anyone watching out for her! There was nobody. Jo leapt down from the hole and ran down the steep hillside. She went as sure-footed as a goat, leaping along till she came to the lane. She crossed it and made her way to the caravan field.

She was just about to go over the stile when she stopped. Julian had said she was to go to the police. But Jo, like the other traveller folk, was afraid of the police.

No traveller ever asked the police for help. Jo felt herself shrivelling up inside when she thought of talking to big policemen.

'No. I'll go to Uncle Fredo,' she thought. 'He will know what to do. I will tell him about it.'

She was going up the field when she saw someone strange there! Who was it? Could it be that horrid man who had tied her up? She had not seen him at all clearly, and she was afraid it might be. She saw that he was talking urgently to some of the fair-folk. They were listening politely, but Jo could see that they thought he was rather mad.

She went a bit nearer, and found that he was asking where Julian and the rest were. He was becoming very angry with the fair people because they assured him that they did not know where the children had gone.

'It's the man they called Pottersham,' said Jo to herself, and dived under a caravan. 'He's come to find out how much we've told anyone about that Face.'

She hid till he had gone away down the hillside to the lane, very red in the face, and shouting out that he would get the police.

Jo crawled out, and the fair-folk crowded round her at once. 'Where have you been? Where are the others?

162

That man wanted to know all about you. He sounds quite mad!'

'He's a *bad* man,' said Jo. 'I'll tell you all about him – and where the others are. We've got to rescue them!'

Whereupon Jo launched into her story with the greatest zest, beginning in the middle, then going back to the beginning, putting in things she had forgotten, and thoroughly muddling everyone. When she ended they all stared at her in excitement. They didn't really know what it was all about but they had certainly gathered a few things.

'You mean to say that those kids are locked up in that tower over there?' said Alfredo, amazed. 'And a spy is with them!'

'No – *he's* not a spy – he's a good man,' explained Jo. 'What they call a scientist, very, very, clever.'

'That man who left just now, he said he was a – a scientist,' said Skippy, stumbling over the unfamiliar word.

'Well, he's a *bad* man,' said Jo, firmly. 'He is probably a spy. He kidnapped the good man, up in the tower there, to take him away to another country. And he tied me up too, like I told you. See my wrists and ankles?'

She displayed them, cut and bruised. The fair-folk looked at them in silence. Then Bufflo cracked his whip and made everyone jump.

'We will rescue them!' he said. 'This is no police job. It is our job.'

'I say, look – that scientist comes back,' said Skippy suddenly. And sure enough, there he was, coming hurriedly up the field to ask some more questions!

'We will get him,' muttered Bufflo. All the fair-folk waited in silence for the man to come up. Then they closed round him solidly and began to walk up the hill. The man was taken with them. He couldn't help himself! He was walked behind a caravan, and before the crowd had come apart again he was on the ground, neatly roped by the rope-man!

'Well, we've got *you*,' said the rope-man. 'And now we'll get on to the next bit of business!'

CHAPTER NINETEEN

Jo joins in

THE 'SCIENTIST', as Skippy persisted in calling him, was put into an empty caravan with windows and doors shut, because he shouted so loudly. When the snake-man opened the door and slid in one of his pythons the scientist stopped shouting at once and lay extremely still.

The snake-man opened the door and his python glided out again. But the man in the caravan had learnt his lesson. Not another sound came from him!

Then everyone in the camp held a conference. There was no hurry about it at all, because it had been decided that nothing should be done before night-time.

'If we make a rescue in the daylight, then the police will come,' said Alfredo. 'They will interfere. They will not believe a word we say. They never do.'

'How shall we rescue them?' said Skippy. 'Do we go through these strange passages and up steep stone stairs? It does not sound nice to me.'

'It isn't at all nice,' Jo assured her. 'And anyway it

wouldn't be sensible. The door leading to the tower room is locked, I told you. And that man has got the key.'

'Ah!' said Bufflo, springing up at once. 'You didn't tell us that before! He has the key? Then I will get it from him!'

'I didn't think of that,' said Jo, watching Bufflo leap up the caravan steps.

He came out in a minute or two and joined them again. 'He has no key on him,' he said. 'He says he never had. He says we are all mad, and he will get the police.'

'He will find it hard to get the police just yet,' said Mrs Alfredo, and gave a high little laugh. 'He has thrown away the key – or given it to a friend, perhaps?'

'Well, it's settled we can't get in through the door that leads to the tower room, then,' said the snake-man, who seemed to have a better grasp of things than the others. 'Right. Is there any other way into the room?'

'Only by the window,' said Jo. 'That slit-window there, see? Too high for any ladder, of course. Anyway, we've got to get into the courtyard first. We'll have to climb over the high castle wall.'

'That is easy,' said the rubber-man. 'I can climb any wall. But not, perhaps, one so high as the tower wall.'

'Can anyone get into or out of the slit of a window?'

asked Bufflo, screwing up his eyes to look at the tower.

'Oh, yes – it's bigger than you think,' said Jo. 'It's very *deep* – the walls are so thick, you see – though I don't think they are so thick up there as they are down below. But Bufflo, how can anyone get up to that window?'

'It can be done,' said Bufflo. 'That is not so difficult! You can lend us a peg-rope, Jekky?' he said to the rope-man.

'Yes,' said Jekky. Jo knew what that was – a thick rope with pegs thrust through the strands to act as footholds.

'But how will you get the peg-rope up?' said Jo, puzzled.

'It can be done,' said Bufflo again, and the talking went on. Jo suddenly began to feel terribly hungry and got up to get herself a meal. When she got back to the conference everything was apparently settled.

'We set off tonight as soon as darkness comes,' Bufflo told her. 'You will not come, Jo. This is man's business.'

'Of course I'm coming!' said Jo, amazed that anyone should think she wasn't. 'They're my friends, aren't they? I'm coming all right!'

'You are not,' said Bufflo, and Jo immediately made

up her mind to disappear before the men set off and hide somewhere so that she might follow them.

By this time it was about six o'clock. Bufflo and the rope-man disappeared into Jekky's caravan and became very busy there. Jo went peeping in at the door to see what they were doing but they ordered her out.

'This is not your business any more,' they said, and turned her out when she refused to go.

When darkness came, a little company set out from the camp. They had searched for Jo to make sure she was not coming, but she had disappeared. Bufflo led the way down the hill, looking extremely large because he was wound about with a great deal of peg-rope. Then came Mr Slither with one of his pythons draped round him. Then the rubber-man with Mr Alfredo.

Bufflo also carried his whip though nobody quite knew why. Anyway, Bufflo always did carry a whip, it was part of him, so nobody questioned him about it.

Behind them, like a little shadow, slipped Jo. What were they going to do? She had watched the tower-window for the last two hours, and when darkness came she saw a light there – a light that shone on and off, on and off.

'That's Dick or Julian signalling,' she thought. 'They will have wondered why I haven't brought help sometime today. They don't know that I was captured and tied up! I'll have something to tell them when we're all together again!'

The little company went over the stile, into the lane and up the path to the castle. They came to the wall. The rubber-man took a jump at it, and literally seemed to run up it, fling himself on to the top, roll over and disappear!

'He's over,' said Bufflo. 'What it is to be made of rubber! I don't believe that fellow ever feels hurt!'

There was a low whistle from the other side of the wall. Bufflo unwound a thin rope from his waist, tied a stone to it and flung it over. The rope slithered after the stone and over the wall like a long thin worm.

Thud! They heard the stone fall on the ground on the other side. Another low whistle told them that the rubber-man had it. Bufflo then undid the peg-rope from his waist, and he and the others held out its length between them, standing one behind the other. One end was fastened to the thin rope whose other end held the stone.

The rubber-man, on the other side of the wall, began to pull on the thin rope. When all the slack was taken in, the peg-rope began to go up the wall too, because it was tied to the thin rope and had to follow it! Up went the peg-rope and up, looking like a great thick caterpillar with tufts sticking out of its sides.

Jo watched. Yes, that was clever. A good and easy way of getting over the thick high wall. But to get the peg-rope up to the slit-window would not be so easy.

A whistle came again. Bufflo let go the peg-rope, and it swung flat against his side of the wall. He tugged it. It was firm. Evidently the rubber-man had tied it fast to something. It was safe to go up. It would bear anyone's weight without slipping down the wall.

Bufflo went up first, using the pegs as footholds and pulling himself up by the rope between the pegs. Each of the men was quick and deft in the way he climbed. Jo waited till the last one had started up, and then leapt for the rope too!

Up she went like a cat and landed beside Bufflo on the other side of the wall. He was astounded and gave her a cuff. She dodged away, and stood aside, watching. She wondered how the men intended to reach the topmost window of the high tower. Perhaps she would be of some help. If only she could be!

The four men stood in the moonlight, looking up at the tower. They talked in low tones, while the rubber-man undid the thin rope from the peg-rope, and neatly coiled it into loops. The peg-rope was left on the wall.

JO JOINS IN

Jo heard a car going up the lane at the bottom of the castle hill. She heard it stop and back somewhere. Part of her attention was on the four men and the other part on the car.

The car stopped its engine. There was no further sound. Jo forgot it for a few minutes, and then was on the alert again – was that voices she heard somewhere? She listened intently. The sound came again on the night air – a low murmur that came nearer.

Jo held her breath – could that horrid man – what was his name – Pottersham – could he have arranged for his equally horrid friends to fetch Mr Terry-Kane and all the children out of the tower that night, and take them off to the coast? Perhaps they had already hired a fishing boat from Joseph the old fisherman, and they would all be away and never heard of again!

So the thoughts ran in Jo's alert mind. Mr Pottersham would have had plenty of time to get fresh orders, and arrange everything before he had gone to the camp and got himself locked up in a caravan! Oh dear – dare she go and warn her Uncle Alfredo, where he stood in the moonlight, holding a little conference with the others?

'He'll cuff me as soon as I go near,' thought Jo, rubbing her left ear, which still stung from Bufflo's cuff. 'They won't listen to me, I know. Still, I'll try.'

She went up to the group of men cautiously. She saw Bufflo take out a dagger-knife from his belt, and tie it to the end of the thin rope that the rubber-man held. She guessed in a moment what he was about to do, and ran to him.

'No, Bufflo, no! Don't throw that knife up – you'll hurt someone – you might wound one of them! No, Bufflo, no!'

'Clear out,' said Bufflo, angrily and raised his hand to slap her. She dodged away.

She went round the group to her uncle. 'Uncle Fredo,' she said, beseechingly, 'listen. I can hear voices – I think those . . .'

Alfredo pushed her away roughly. 'Will you stop this, Jo? Do you want a good punishing? You behave like a buzzing fly!'

Mr Slither called her. 'See here, Jo – if you want to be useful, hold Beauty for me. He will be in the way in a minute.'

He draped the great snake over her shoulders, and Beauty hissed loudly. He began to coil himself round Jo, and she caught hold of his tail. She liked Beauty, but just at that moment she didn't want him at all!

She stood back and watched what Bufflo was going to do. She knew, of course, and her heart beat fearfully.

He was going to throw his knife through that high slit-window, a thing that surely only Bufflo, with his unerring aim, could possibly do!

'But if he gets it through the window, it may stick into one of the four up there – or into Mr Terry-Kane,' she thought, in a panic. 'It might wound Dick – or Timmy! Oh, I wish Bufflo wouldn't do it!'

She heard low voices again – this time they came from just the other side of the wall! Men were going to follow those secret passages, and go right up to the tower room! Jo knew they were! They would be there before Bufflo and the others had followed out their rescue plan. She pictured the four children being dragged down the stairs, and Terry-Kane, too. Would Timmy defend them? He would – but the men would certainly deal with him. They knew there was a dog there, because Timmy had barked the night before.

'Oh, dear,' thought Jo, in despair. 'I must do something! But what can I DO?'

CHAPTER TWENTY

A lot of excitement

JO SUDDENLY made up her mind. She would follow the men through those passages, and see if she could warn the others by shouting when she came near enough to the tower room. She would help them *somehow*. Bufflo and the others would be too late to save them now.

Jo ran to the wall. She was up the peg-rope left there and down the other side in a trice. She made her way to where the missing stone left the gap in the old wall.

Beauty, the python, was surprised to find himself pulled off and thrown on the ground, just before Jo ran for the wall. He wasn't used to that sort of treatment. He lay there, coiling and uncoiling himself. Where had that nice girl gone? Beauty liked Jo – she knew how to treat him!

He glided after her. He too went up the wall and over, quite easily, though he did not need to use the peg-rope like Jo. He glided after Jo quickly. It was amazing to see his speed when he really wanted to be quick!

A LOT OF EXCITEMENT

He came to the hole in the wall. Ah, he liked holes. He glided in after Jo. He caught up with her just as she had reached the end of the small passage, through which she had had to walk bent double. He pushed against her legs and then twined himself round her.

She gave a small scream, and then realised what it was. 'Beauty! You'll get into trouble with Mr Slither, coming after me like this. Go back! Stop twining yourself round me – I've got important things to do.'

But Beauty was not like Timmy. He obeyed only when he thought he would, and he was not going to obey this time!

'All right – come with me if you want to,' said Jo, at last, having in vain tried to push the great snake back. 'You'll be company, I suppose. Stop hissing like that, Beauty! You sound like an engine letting off steam in this narrow passage.'

Soon Jo had gone down the steep steps that led to the level passage under the courtyard. Beauty slithered down them too, rather surprised at the sudden drop. Along the wider passage they went, Beauty now in front, and Jo sometimes tripping over his powerful tail.

Up steps again, and into the thick wall of the castle itself. Something shining ahead made Jo suddenly stop. She listened but heard nothing. She went forward cautiously and found that in the little secret room was a small lantern, left there probably by one of the men in front.

She saw the rusty dagger lying on the floor where she had left it the night before and grinned. The rope was there too, that she had untied from her arms and legs.

Jo went on, along the passage that led to the spiral stairway. Now she thought she could hear something. She climbed the steep stairs, cross with Beauty because he pushed by her and almost sent her headlong down them. She came to the door that opened on to the little gallery. Dare she open it? Suppose the men were just outside?

She opened it slowly. It was pitch dark on the other side, of course, but Jo knew she was about to step out on the little gallery. Beauty suddenly slithered up her and coiled himself lovingly round her. Jo could not make the snake uncoil, and she stepped out on the small gallery with Beauty firmly wrapped about her.

And then, what a noise she heard! She stood quite aghast. Whatever could be going on? She heard excited voices – surely one was Bufflo's? And was that crack a pistol-shot?

What had happened down below in the courtyard when Jo had disappeared over the wall with Beauty?

None of the men noticed her go. They were all too intent on their plan.

Bufflo was to use his gift for knife-throwing – but in quite a different way from usual! He was to throw the knife high into the air, and make it curve in through the slit-window at the top of the tower!

Bufflo was an expert at knife-throwing, or, indeed, at any kind of throwing. He stood there in the courtyard, looking up at the high window. He half-closed his eyes, getting the distance and the direction fixed in his mind. The moon suddenly went in, and he lowered his hand. He could not throw accurately in the dark!

The moon sailed out again, quite brilliant. Bufflo lost no time. Once more he took aim, his eyes narrowed – and then the knife flew high into the air, gleaming as it went – taking behind it a long tail of very thin rope.

It struck the sill of the slit-window and fell back. Bufflo caught it deftly. The moonlight showed plainly that the knife was not sharp-pointed – Bufflo had filed off the point, and it was now quite blunt. Jo need not have worried about someone in the tower being hurt by a sharp dagger!

Once more Bufflo took aim, and once more the knife sailed up, swift as a swallow, shining silver as it went. This time it fell cleanly in at the window-opening, slithered all the way across the stone ledge inside, and fell to the floor of the tower room with a thud.

It caused the greatest astonishment there. Mr Terry-Kane, the four children and Timmy were all huddled together for warmth in one corner. They were hungry and cold. No one had brought them food, and they had nothing to keep them warm except a rug belonging to Terry-Kane. All that day they had been in the tower room, sometimes looking from the window, sometimes shouting all together at the tops of their voices. But nobody heard them, and nobody saw them.

'Why doesn't Jo bring help?' they had said a hundred times that long, long day. They didn't know that poor Jo was spending hours trying to free herself from the knots round her legs and wrists.

They had looked out of the window at the camp on the opposite hill, where the fair-folk went about their business, looking like ants on the far-off green slope. Was Jo there? It was too far-off to make out anyone for certain.

When darkness came Julian had flashed his torch from the window on and off – on and off. Then, cold and miserable, they had all huddled together, with Timmy licking first one and then another, not at all understanding why they should stay in this one room.

'Timmy will be so thirsty,' said George. 'He keeps licking round his mouth in the way he does when he wants a drink.'

'Well, I feel like licking round *my* mouth too,' said Dick.

They were half asleep when the knife came thudding into the room. Timmy leapt up at once and barked madly. He stood and stared at the knife that lay gleaming in the moonlight, and barked without stopping.

'A knife!' said George, in amazement. 'A knife with a string tied on the end!'

'It's blunt,' said Julian, picking it up. 'The tip has been filed off. What's the meaning of it? And why the string tied to it?'

'Be careful that another knife doesn't come through,' warned Terry-Kane.

'It won't,' said Julian. 'I think this is something to do with Jo. She hasn't gone to the police. She has got the fair-folk to help us. This is Bufflo's knife, I'm sure!'

They were all round him, examining it now. 'I'm going to the window,' said Julian. 'I'll look right out into the courtyard. Hold my legs, Dick.'

He climbed up on the stone sill and crawled a little forward through the deep-set slit. He came to the outer edge of the window and looked down. Dick hung on to his legs, afraid that the sill might crumble away and Julian would fall.

'I can see four people down in the courtyard,' said Julian. 'Oh, good – one is Alfredo, one is Bufflo – and I can't make out the other two. AHOY down there!'

The four men below were standing looking up intently. They saw Julian's head appear outside the window, and waved to him.

'Pull in the rope!' shouted Bufflo. He had now tied the end of a second peg-rope to the thin rope, and he and the others lifted it so that it might run easily up the wall.

Julian slid back into the tower room. He was excited. 'This string on the knife runs down the wall and is tied to a thicker rope,' he said. 'I'll pull it up – and up will come a rope that we can climb down!'

He pulled on the string, and more and more of it appeared through the window. Then Julian felt a heavier weight and he guessed the thicker rope was coming up. Now he had to pull more slowly. Dick helped him.

Over the windowsill, in at the window, appeared the first length of the peg-rope. The children had never seen one like it before, they were used to the more ordinary rope-ladder. But Terry-Kane knew what it was.

A LOT OF EXCITEMENT

'A peg-rope,' he said. 'Circus people and fair people make them – they are lighter and easier to manage than rope-ladders. We'll have to fix the end to something really strong, so that it will hold our weight.'

Anne looked at the peg-rope in dismay. She didn't at all like the idea of climbing down that, swinging on it all the way down the high stone wall of the tower! But the others looked at it with pleasure and excitement – a way of escape – a good, strong rope to climb down out of this hateful cold room!

Terry-Kane looked about for something to fasten the rope to. In the wall at one side was a great iron ring, embedded in the stone. What it had been used for once upon a time nobody could imagine – but certainly it would be of great use now!

There were no pegs in the first yard or so of the rope. Terry-Kane and Julian cut off the string that had pulled it up, and then dragged it right through until the first peg stopped it. Then they twisted the rope-end round upon itself and made great strong knots that could not slip.

Julian took hold of the rope, and leant back hard on it, pulling it with all his strength. 'It would hold a dozen of us at once!' he said, pleased. 'Shall I go first, sir? I can help everyone else down then, if I'm at the bottom. Dick

181

and you can see to the girls when they climb out.'

'What about Timmy?' asked George, at once.

'We'll wrap him up in the rug, tie him firmly and lower him down on the string,' said Dick. 'It's very strong string – thin rope, really.'

'I'll go down now,' said Julian, and went to the window. Then he stopped. Someone was clattering up the stone steps that led to the tower. Someone was at the door! Who could it be?

CHAPTER TWENTY-ONE

In the tower room

THE DOOR was flung open, and a man stood there, panting. Behind him came three others.

'Pottersham!' said Terry-Kane. 'So you're back!'

'Yes. I'm back,' said the panting man.

Timmy began to bark and try to escape from George's hand. He showed his teeth and all his hackles rose up on his neck. He looked a very savage dog indeed.

Pottersham backed away. He didn't like the look of Timmy at all! 'If you let that dog go, I'll shoot him,' he said, and as if by magic a gun appeared in his right hand.

George tried her hardest to restrain the furious Timmy, and called to Julian to help her. 'Julian, hold him as well. He'll fling himself on that man, he's so angry.'

Julian went to help. Between them they forced the furious dog back into a corner, where George tried in vain to pacify him. She was terrified that he might be shot.

'You can't behave like this, Pottersham,' began

Terry-Kane, but he was cut short.

'We've no time to lose. We're taking you, Terry-Kane, and one of the kids. We can use him for a hostage if too much fuss is made about your disappearance. We'll take this boy,' and he grabbed at Dick. Dick gave him a punch on the jaw immediately, thanking his stars that he had learnt boxing at school. But he at once found himself on the floor! These men were not standing for any nonsense. They were in a hurry!

'Get him,' said Pottersham, to one of the men behind him, and Dick was pounced on. Then Terry-Kane was taken too, and his arms held behind him.

'What about these other kids?' he said, angrily. 'You're surely not going to lock them up in this room and leave them.'

'Yes, we are,' said Pottersham. 'We're leaving a note for the old turnstile woman to tell her they're up here. Let the police rescue them if they can!'

'You always were a . . .' began Terry-Kane, and then ducked to avoid a blow.

Timmy barked madly all the time, and almost choked himself trying to get away from George and Julian. He was mad with rage, and when he saw Dick being roughly treated he very nearly did manage to get loose. 'Take them,' ordered Pottersham. 'And hurry.

Go on – down the steps with them.'

The three men forced Terry-Kane and Dick to the stone stairs – and then everyone shot round in astonishment! A loud voice suddenly came from the window!

Anne gasped. Bufflo was there! He hadn't been able to understand why nobody came down the peg-rope, so he had come up to find out. And to his enormous surprise there appeared to be quite an upset going on!

'Hey there! WHAT'S UP?' he yelled, and slid into the room, looking most out of place with his mop of yellow hair, bright checked shirt and whip!

'BUFFLO!' shouted all four of the children, and Timmy changed his angry bark to a welcoming one. Terry-Kane looked on in astonishment, his arms still pinioned behind him.

'Who in the world is this?' shouted Pottersham, alarmed at Bufflo's sudden appearance through the window. 'How did he get through there?'

Bufflo eyed the gun in Pottersham's hand and lazily cracked his small whip once or twice. 'Put that thing away,' he said, in his drawling voice. 'You ought to know better than to wave a thing like that about when there's kids around. Go on – put it away!'

He cracked his whip again. Pottersham pointed the

gun at him angrily. And then a most amazing thing happened.

The gun disappeared from Pottersham's hand, flew right up into the air, and was neatly caught by Bufflo! And all by the crack of a whip!

Crack! Just that – and the gun had been flicked from his hand by the powerful lash-end – and had stung Pottersham's fingers so much he was now howling in pain and bending double to nurse his injured hand.

Terry-Kane gasped. What a neat trick – but how dangerous! The gun might have gone off. Now the tables were indeed turned, for it was Bufflo who held the gun, not Pottersham. And Pottersham looked very pale indeed!

He stared as if he hardly knew what to do. 'Let go of them,' ordered Bufflo, nodding his head towards Terry-Kane and Dick. The three men released them and stood back.

'Seems as if we got to get the police after all,' remarked Bufflo, in a perfectly ordinary voice, as if these happenings were not at all unusual. 'You can let that dog go now, if you want, Julian.'

'No! NO!' cried Pottersham in terror – and at that moment the moon went behind a cloud, and the tower room was plunged in darkness – except for the lantern that Pottersham had set down on the floor when he had first arrived.

He saw one slight chance for himself and the others. He suddenly kicked the lantern, which flew into the air and hit Bufflo, then went out, and left the entire place in pitch darkness. Bufflo did not dare to fire. He might hit the wrong person!

'Set the dog loose!' he roared – but it was too late. By the time Timmy had got to the door, it was slammed shut – and the bolt was shot home on the other side! There was the sound of hurried steps slipping and stumbling down the stone stairway in the dark.

'Hrrr!' said Bufflo, when the moon came out again, and showed him the astonished and dismayed faces of the five in the room. 'We slipped up somewhere, didn't we? They've gone!'

'Yes. But without *us*,' said Terry-Kane, letting Dick untie his arms. 'They've probably gone down through those passages. They'll be out before we've escaped ourselves, more's the pity. And now we've got to try this rope trick down the tower wall, seeing that the door is locked!'

'Come on, then,' said Julian. 'Let's go before anything else happens.' He went to the window, slid to the outer edge, and took hold of the rope. It was perfectly easy to climb down, though it wasn't very pleasant to look below him into the courtyard. It seemed so very far away.

Anne went next, very much afraid, but not showing it. She was quite a good climber so she didn't find the rope difficult. She was very, very glad when she at last stood safely beside Julian.

Then came George, with a bit of news. 'I can't think what's happening to the four men,' she said. 'They still seem to be about – and they're yelling like anything. It sounds as if they are rushing round that gallery that runs along the walls of the tower room below.'

'Well, let them,' said Julian. 'If they stay there long enough, we'll have time to go to the hole in the outer wall, and wait for them to come out one by one! That would be very, very nice.'

'Timmy's coming now,' said George. 'I've wrapped him up well in that rug and tied it all round him, and put a kind of rope harness on him. Dick's going to lower him down. We doubled the rope to make sure it would hold. Look – here he comes! Poor darling Timmy! He can't think what in the world is happening!'

Timmy came down slowly, swinging a little, and bumping into the stone wall now and again. He gave a little yelp each time, and George was sure he would be covered with bruises! She watched in great suspense as he came lower and lower.

'Timmy ought to be used to this sort of thing by now,' said Julian. 'He's had plenty of it in the adventures he's shared with us. Hey there, Tim! Slowly does it! Good dog, then! I guess you're glad to be standing on firm ground again!'

Timmy certainly was. He allowed himself to be untied from his rug by George, and then tried a few steps to see if the ground was really firm beneath his feet. He leapt up at George joyfully, very glad to be out in the open air again.

'Here comes Dick,' said Julian. The peg-rope swayed a little, and Alfredo went to hold it steady. He and the rubber-man and Mr Slither were now extremely concerned about something, so concerned that they had hardly a word to say to Julian and George and Anne.

They had suddenly missed Jo and the snake! The snake-man didn't care tuppence about Jo – but he did care about his precious, beloved, magnificent python! He had already hunted all round the courtyard for it.

'If Jo's taken it back to camp with her, I'll pull her hair off!' muttered the snake-man, unhappily, and Julian looked at him in astonishment. What *was* he muttering about?

Terry-Kane came next, and last of all, Bufflo, who seemed to slide down in a most remarkable way, not using the pegs at all. He leapt down beside them, grinning.

'There's a tremendous upset up aloft!' he said. 'Yelling and shouting and scampering about. What do you suppose is the matter with those fellows? We'll be able to get them nicely, if we go to the hole in the wall. They'll be out there soon, I reckon. Come on!'

CHAPTER TWENTY-TWO

Beauty and Jo enjoy themselves

SOMETHING CERTAINLY had happened to upset Pottersham and his three friends. After the door of the tower room had been slammed and bolted, the men had gone clattering down the stone steps. They had come to the door that led into the gallery, and had opened it and gone out on to the gallery itself.

But before they could find the spiral staircase a little way along, Pottersham had tripped over something – something that hissed like an engine letting off steam, and had wound itself round his legs.

He yelled, and struck out at whatever it was. At first he had thought it was a man lying in wait for him, who had pounced at his legs – but he knew it wasn't a man now. No man could hiss like that!

One of the men shone a torch down to see what was the matter with Pottersham. What he saw made him yell and almost drop the torch.

'A snake! A snake bigger than any I've ever seen! It's got you, Pottersham!'

'Help me, man, help me!' shouted Pottersham, hitting down at the snake as hard as he could. 'It's squeezing my legs together in its coils.'

The other men ran to help him. As soon as they began to tug, Beauty uncoiled and glided off into the shadows.

'Where's the horrible thing gone?' panted Pottersham. 'It nearly crushed my legs to powder! Quick, let's go before it comes back. Where in the world did it come from?'

They took a few steps – but the snake was lying in wait for them! It tripped them all up by gliding in and out of their legs, and then began to coil itself round one of the men's waists.

Such a shouting and yelling and howling began then! If ever there were frightened men, those four were! No matter where they went, that snake seemed to be there, coiling and uncoiling, gliding, writhing, squeezing!

It was Jo who had set the python on to them, of course. Jo had stayed in the gallery while all the disturbance upstairs had been going on, Beauty draped round her neck. The girl tried in vain to make out what was happening.

And then she had heard a door slam, a bolt shot home, and men's feet pouring down the stone stairs! She guessed it must be the four whose voices she had heard earlier in the evening, the men who had gone through the passage.

'Beauty! Now it's *your* turn to do something,' said Jo, and she pulled the snake off her shoulders. He poured himself down her and flowed on to the ground in one beautiful movement. He glided towards the men, who were now coming out of the gallery. After that, the python had the time of his life. The more the men howled the more excited the big snake became.

Jo was huddled in a corner, laughing till the tears ran down her cheeks. She knew the snake was quite harmless unless he gave one of the men too tight a squeeze. She couldn't see what was going on, but she could hear.

'Oh dear – there's another one down!' she thought, as she heard one of the men tripped up by Beauty. 'And there goes another! I shall die of laughing. Good old Beauty! He's never allowed to behave like this in the usual way. He *must* be enjoying himself!'

At last the men could bear it no more. 'Come up to that tower room!' yelled Pottersham. 'I'm not going back through those dark passages with snakes after me. There must be dozens of them here. We'll be bitten soon!'

Jo laughed out loud. Dozens of them! Well, probably Beauty did seem like a dozen snakes to the bewildered men falling over one another in the dark. But Beauty would not bite – he was not poisonous.

Somehow the men got up into the tower room, and left the snake behind. Beauty was tired of the game now, and went to Jo when the girl called to him. She draped him round her neck, and listened.

The door up in the tower room had slammed. Jo slipped up the steps, felt for the door-bolt in the darkness and neatly and quietly pulled it across. Now, unless the men liked to risk going down the peg-rope, which she guessed Bufflo had put up against the wall to rescue the others, they were nicely trapped. And if they *did* go down the rope they would be sure to find a few people waiting for them at the bottom!

'Come on, Beauty, let's go,' said Jo, and went down the steps, wishing she had a torch. She remembered the little lantern that had been left in the hidden room, and felt more cheerful. She would be able to take that with her down all those dark passages. Good!

Beauty slithered in front of her. He knew the way all right! They came to the little room, and Jo thankfully picked up the lantern. She looked down at the big python and he stared up at her with gleaming, unwinking eyes. His long body coiled and uncoiled, shining brown and polished in the light.

'I wouldn't mind you for a pet, if you were a bit smaller,' Jo told him. 'I don't know why people don't like snakes. Oh, Beauty – it makes me laugh to think of the way you treated those men!'

She chuckled as she went along the secret ways, holding the lantern high, except when she came to the last passage of all, and had to walk bent double. Beauty waited for her when she came to the hole in the wall. He had heard noises outside.

Jo climbed out first, and was immensely surprised to find herself pounced on and held. She wriggled and shouted and struggled, and finally bit the hand that was holding her.

Then a torch was shone on her and a shout went up. 'It's Jo! Jo, where have you been? And look here, if you bite like that I'll scrag you!'

'Bufflo! I'm sorry – but what did you want to go and pounce on me for?' cried Jo. The moon suddenly came out and lit up the scene. She saw Julian and the rest there, coming up eagerly.

'Jo! Are you all right?' said her uncle. 'We were worried about you. Where have you been?'

Jo took no notice. She ran up to Dick and the others. 'You escaped!' she cried. 'Did you all get safely down the peg-rope?'

'There's no time to tell about that now,' said Bufflo, watching the hole in the wall. 'What about those fellows? We're waiting for them here. Did you hear anything of them, Jo?'

'Oh, yes. I followed them. Oh, Bufflo, it was so funny . . .' said Jo, and began to laugh. Bufflo shook her, but she couldn't stop. And then who should come gliding out through the hole but Beauty!

Mr Slither saw him at once and gave a yell. 'Beauty! Jo, did you take him with you? You wicked girl! Come here, my Beauty!'

The snake glided to him and wound himself lovingly round him.

'I'm not wicked,' said Jo, indignantly. 'Beauty wanted to come with me and he did – and oh, he got mixed up with all those men, and . . .'

She went off into peals of laughter again. Dick grinned in sympathy. Jo was very funny when she couldn't stop laughing.

Alfredo shook her roughly and made her stop. 'Tell us what you know about those men,' he commanded. 'Are they coming out this way? Where are they?'

'Oh – the men,' said Jo, wiping her eyes and trying to stop laughing. 'They're all right. Beauty chased them back to the tower room, and I bolted them in. They're

BEAUTY AND JO ENJOY THEMSELVES

still there, I expect – unless they dare to get down the peg-rope, which I bet they won't!'

Bufflo gave a short laugh. 'You did well, Jo,' he said. 'You and Beauty!'

He gave a sharp order to Alfredo and the rubber-man, who went back over the wall and into the courtyard to watch if the men slid down the peg-rope.

'I think it would be a good idea to get the police now,' said Terry-Kane, beginning to feel that he must be in some kind of extraordinary dream, with peg-ropes and whips and knives and snakes turning up in such a peculiar manner. 'That fellow Pottersham is dangerous. He's a traitor, and must be caught before he gives away all that he knows about the work he and I have been doing.'

'Right,' said Bufflo. 'We've got another fellow locked up too – in an empty caravan.'

'But – didn't he escape, then?' said Jo, surprised. 'I thought that man Pottersham, who's up in the tower room now, was the one we locked up.'

'The one we locked up is *still* locked up,' said Bufflo grimly.

'But who is *he*, then?' said Terry-Kane, bewildered.

'We'll soon find out,' said Bufflo. 'Come on, let's get going now. It's very late, you kids must be dying of hunger, somebody ought to go to the police, and I want to get back to camp.'

'Alfredo and the rubber-man will keep guard on the peg-rope,' said Mr Slither, still fondling Beauty. 'There is no need to stay here any longer.'

So down the hill they went, talking nineteen to the dozen. Terry-Kane went off to the police station and to telephone what he vaguely called 'the high-up authorities'. The five children began to think hungrily of something to eat and drink! Timmy ran to the stream as soon as they reached the field and began to lap thirstily.

'Let's just find out if you know the fellow we've got locked up in this caravan,' said Bufflo, when they got to the camp. 'He seems the only unexplained bit so far.'

He unlocked the caravan, and called loudly: 'Come on out. We want to know who you are!' He held up a lamp, and the man inside came slowly to the door.

There was a shout of amazement from all the children. 'Uncle Quentin!' cried Julian, Dick and Anne. 'Father!' shouted George. 'What ARE you doing here?'

CHAPTER TWENTY-THREE

Having a wonderful time!

THERE WAS a minute or two of silence. Everyone was most astonished. To think that George's father had been locked up like that! It had been Jo's mistake, of course – she had been so sure he was Mr Pottersham.

'Julian,' said Uncle Quentin, very much on his dignity, and also very angry, 'I must ask you to go and get the police here. I was set on and locked up in this caravan for no reason at all.'

Bufflo began to look most disturbed. He turned on Jo.

'Why didn't you tell us he was George's father?' he said.

'I didn't know it *was*,' said Jo. 'I've never seen him, and anyhow I thought ...'

'It doesn't matter what you thought,' said Uncle Quentin, looking at the little girl in disgust. 'I insist on the police being fetched.'

'Uncle Quentin, I'm sure it's all been a mistake,' said Julian, 'and anyway Mr Terry-Kane has gone to the police himself.'

His uncle stared at him as if he couldn't believe his ears. '*Terry-Kane?* Where is he? What has happened? Is he found?'

'Yes. It's rather a long story,' said Julian. 'It all began when we saw that face at the window. I told Aunt Fanny all about that, Uncle, and she said she would tell you when you got back from London. Well – it *was* Mr Terry-Kane at the window!'

'I thought so! I told your Aunt Fanny I had a feeling it was!' said his uncle. 'That's why I came as soon as ever I could – but you were none of you here. What happened to you?'

'Well, that's part of the story, Uncle,' said Julian, patiently. 'But I say, do you mind if we have something to eat? We're practically dead from starvation – haven't had anything since yesterday!'

That ended the interview for the time being! Mrs Alfredo bustled about, and soon there was a perfectly glorious meal set in front of the five half-starved children. They sat round a camp-fire and ate and ate and ate.

Mrs Alfredo practically emptied her big pot for them. Timmy was surrounded by plates of scraps and big bones brought by every member of the camp!

HAVING A WONDERFUL TIME!

Almost every minute someone loomed up out of the darkness with a plate of something or other either for the hungry children, or for Timmy.

At last they really could eat no more, and Julian began to tell their extraordinary story. Dick took it up, and George added quite a few bits. Jo interrupted continually and even Timmy put in a few barks. Only Anne said nothing. She was leaning against her uncle, fast asleep.

'I never heard such a tale in my life,' said Uncle Quentin, continually. 'Never! Fancy that fellow Pottersham going off with Terry-Kane like that. I *knew* Terry-Kane was all right – *he* wouldn't let his country down. Now, Pottersham I never did like. Well, go on.'

The fair-folk were as enthralled as Uncle Quentin with the tale. They came closer and closer as the story of the secret passages, the hidden room, the stone stairways and the rest was unfolded.

They got very excited when they learnt how Bufflo had appeared in the tower room and had flicked the gun out of Pottersham's hand. Uncle Quentin threw back his head and roared when he heard that bit.

'What a shock for that fellow!' he said. 'I'd like to have seen his face. Well, well – I never heard such a tale in my life!'

And then it was Jo's turn to tell how she had followed the four men into the secret passages, and had set Beauty, the python, on to the men. She began to laugh again as she told her tale, and soon all the fair-folk were laughing in sympathy, rocking to and fro, with tears streaming down their faces.

Only Uncle Quentin looked rather solemn at this point. He remembered how he had felt when, because of his shouting, the fair-folk had sent the python into his caravan, and almost frightened him out of his life.

'Mr Slither, please do get Beauty,' begged Jo. 'He ought to listen to his part of the story. He was wonderful. He enjoyed it all too. I'm sure he would have laughed if only snakes *could* laugh.'

Poor Uncle Quentin didn't like to object when the snake-man fetched his beloved python – in fact, he fetched both of them, and they had never had such a fuss made of them before. They were patted and rubbed and pulled about in a way they both seemed to enjoy hugely.

'Let me hold Beauty, Mr Slither,' said Jo, at last, and she draped him round her neck like a long, shiny scarf. Uncle Quentin looked as if he was going to be sick. He would certainly have got up and gone away if it hadn't been that his favourite niece Anne was fast asleep against his shoulder.

'What extraordinary people George seems to be friends with,' he thought. 'I suppose they are all right – but really! What with whips and knives and snakes I must say I find all this very peculiar.'

'Somebody's coming up the field,' said Jo, suddenly. 'It's – yes, it's Mr Terry-Kane, and he's got three policemen with him.'

Immediately almost all the fair-folk melted away into the darkness. They knew quite well why the police had come – not for them, but because of Mr Pottersham and his unpleasant friends. But all the same they wanted nothing to do with the three burly policemen walking up the hill with Terry-Kane.

Uncle Quentin leapt to his feet as soon as he saw Terry-Kane. He ran to meet him joyfully, and pumped his arm up and down, up and down, shaking hands so vigorously that Terry-Kane felt quite exhausted.

'My dear fellow,' said Uncle Quentin, 'I'm so glad you're safe. I told everyone you weren't a traitor, and never could be – everyone! I went up to London and told them. I'm glad you're all right.'

'Well – it's thanks to these children,' said Terry-Kane, who looked very tired. 'I expect you've heard the peculiar and most extraordinary tale of the face at the window.'

'Yes – it's all so extraordinary that I shouldn't believe it if I read it in a book,' said Uncle Quentin. 'And yet it all happened! My dear fellow, you must be very tired!'

'I am,' said Terry-Kane. 'But I'm not going to lie down and sleep until those other fellows are safely under lock and key – Pottersham and his fine friends! Do you mind if I leave you for a bit, and go off to the castle again? We simply must catch those fellows. I came to ask if one of the children could go with us, because I hear we have to creep through all kinds of passages and galleries and up spiral stairways and goodness knows what.'

'But – didn't *you* go that way when Pottersham first took you there and hid you in that room?' asked Dick, surprised.

'Yes. I must have gone that way,' said Mr Terry-Kane. 'But I was blindfolded and half-doped with something they had made me drink. I've no idea of the way. Of course, Pottersham knew every inch – he's written books about all these old castles, you know – nobody knows more about them and their secrets than he does. He certainly put his knowledge to good use this week!'

'I'll go with you,' said Jo. 'I've been up and down those passages four times now. I know them by heart! The others have only been once.'

'Yes, you go,' said Bufflo.

'Take Timmy,' said George most generously, for usually she would never let Timmy go with Jo.

'Or take a snake,' suggested Dick, with a grin.

'I won't take anything,' said Jo. 'I'll be all right with three big policemen! So long as they're not after *me*, I like them!'

She didn't really, but she couldn't help boasting a little. She set off with Terry-Kane and the three policemen, strutting a little, and feeling quite a heroine.

The others all went to their caravans, tired out. Uncle Quentin sat by the camp-fire, waiting for the arrival of Pottersham and his three friends.

'Good night,' said Julian to the girls. 'I'd like to wait till the crowd come back – complete with the rubber-man and Alfredo – but I shall fall asleep standing on my feet in a minute. I say, wasn't that a smashing supper?'

'Super!' said the others. 'Well – see you tomorrow.'

They all slept very late the next day. Jo was back long before they awoke, very anxious to tell them how they had captured Pottersham and the others, and how they had been marched off to the police station, with her following all the way. But Mrs Alfredo would not let her wake the four children up.

However, they did awake at last, and got up eagerly, remembering all the exciting moments of the day before. Soon they were jumping down the steps of the two caravans, eager to hear the latest news.

'Hallo, Father!' shouted George, seeing him not far off.

'Hallo, Uncle Quentin! Hallo, Jo!' called the others, and soon heard the latest bits of information from Jo who was very proud of being in at the finish.

'But they didn't put up any fight at all,' she said, rather disappointed. 'I think Beauty scared all the fight out of them last night – they just gave in without a word.'

'Now you children!' called Mrs Alfredo, 'I have kept a little breakfast for you. You like to come?'

They did like to come! Jo went too, though she had already had one breakfast. Uncle Quentin went to sit down with them. He gazed around amazed at all the goings-on of the camp.

Bufflo was doing some remarkable rope-spinning and whip-cracking. The rubber-man was wriggling in and out of the wheel-spokes of his caravan without stopping.

HAVING A WONDERFUL TIME!

Mr Slither was polishing his snakes. Dacca was step-dancing on a board, click-click-clickity-click.

Alfredo came up with his buttonhook-like torches, and his metal bowl. 'I give you a treat,' he announced to Uncle Quentin. 'You would like to see me fire-eat?'

Uncle Quentin stared at him as if he thought he had gone raving mad.

'He's a fire-eater, Uncle,' explained Dick.

'Oh. No, thank you, my good man. I would rather not see you eat fire,' said Uncle Quentin, politely but very firmly. Alfredo was most disappointed. He had meant to give this man a real treat to make up for locking him into the caravan! He went away sadly, and Mrs Alfredo screamed after him.

'You foolish man. Who wants to see you fire-eat? You have no brains. You are a big, silly bad man. You keep away with your fire-eating!' She disappeared into her caravan, and Uncle Quentin looked after her, astonished at her sudden outburst.

'This is really a very extraordinary place,' he said. 'And *most* extraordinary people. I'm going back home today, George. Wouldn't you all like to come with me? I don't really feel it's the right thing for you to get mixed up in so many funny doings.'

'Oh *no*, Father,' said George, in horror. 'Go home

when we've only just settled in! Of *course* not. None of us wants to leave – do we, Julian?' she said, looking round beseechingly at him.

Julian answered at once. 'George is right, Uncle. We're just beginning to enjoy ourselves here. I think we're *all* agreed on that!'

'We are,' said everyone, and Timmy thumped his tail hard and gave a very loud 'WOOF'.

'Very well,' said Uncle Quentin, getting up. 'I must go, I suppose. I'll catch the bus down to the station. Come down with me.'

They went to see him off on the bus. It came up well on time and he got in.

'Goodbye,' he said. 'What message shall I give your mother, George? She'll expect to hear something from the five of you.'

'Well,' shouted everyone, as the bus rumbled off, 'well – just tell her the FIVE ARE HAVING A WONDERFUL TIME! Goodbye, Uncle Quentin, goodbye!'

Join the adventure!

If you can't wait to explore further with
FAMOUS FIVE, read the next book in the series:

Get to know Julian

Julian is tall and good-looking with a determined face and brown eyes. He is the oldest of the Five (twelve years old when we first meet him) and he sees himself as the leader. Sometimes he can be over-protective – in *Five Go Off in a Caravan*, he suggests locking Anne and George in their caravan at night for their safety. (George replies that Timmy is far better protection than any lock.) Julian gets on well with adults, as he has 'a polite, well-mannered way with him that all grown-ups liked'. He is helpful and caring to those in need but keen to help the police track down villains. He has a quick tongue and can offer sharp words to nasty adults who try to cross him.

Other people say

That made George laugh, though she didn't want to. It was really impossible to sulk with good-tempered Julian.

I'd bank on Julian to keep the others in order and see they were all safe and sound.

Julian says

You know – I've got a sort of plan coming into my head. Wait a bit – don't interrupt me. I'm thinking

Get to know Dick

Dick is Julian and Anne's eleven-year-old brother. When he was little, he was a bit of a cry-baby but he has grown into a brave and competent boy. Don't be surprised if it's Dick who spots the clue or detail that leads to solving a mystery. He can still be a joker, though, and has a great sense of humour. You'll sometimes find him making fun of Julian when he's being too serious, and he's good at winning over George. Dick is usually hungry and does not like to miss a meal – perhaps it's because of him that wonderful food features so often in the books.

Dick says

I wonder what sort of a tutor Uncle Quentin will choose. If only he would choose the right kind – someone jolly and full of fun, who knows that holiday lessons are sickening to have, and tries to make up for them by being a sport out of lesson-time.

Let's have our dinner!

Other people say

You're a brick! A real brick!

Get to know Anne

Anne is the ten-year-old sister of Julian and Dick. She likes wearing dresses and playing with dolls but in other ways is similar to her cousin George. Just like George, Anne puts other people first and prides herself on her honesty. She likes horse riding and becomes captain of games at her school. It has to be said, though, that Anne isn't a fan of adventures – although she's good at organising her siblings and cousin, and sorting out meals and other arrangements wherever she happens to be. Although she is quiet she won't always let others get the better of her – Julian once described her as changing from a mouse into a tiger.

Anne says

You know, most of our hols have been packed with adventures - awfully exciting, I know - but I'd like an ordinary holiday now, wouldn't you - not too exciting.

Other people say

Anne has been at work – you know how she loves to put everything in its place. We don't need to worry about anything when she's about. Good old Anne!

Get to know George

Don't try to call George by her proper name, Georgina – she hates it. In fact, she wishes she were a boy and will never wear dresses. She is an only child who lives with her parents Quentin and Fanny. At the start of the series, she is often moody and sulky because she doesn't think she needs friends, just Timothy, her beloved dog. (If ever she's scared, it's for Timmy's sake, not her own safety.) But as she gets to know her cousins, she warms to them and enjoys being part of a group. George has short, curly hair and blue eyes. She loves outdoor activities, like swimming and climbing. She is extremely honest and kind at heart, but that fiery personality is here to stay.

Other people say

George says

Who can stop George doing what she wants to!

If a person doesn't like dogs, especially a dog like our Timothy, then there really must be something wrong with him.

I don't make friends with people just because they're my cousins, or something silly like that. I only make friends with people if I like them.

Get to know Timothy

Timothy is a big, brown mongrel dog. He is George's soulmate – they've been inseparable since she found him as a puppy on the moor. But for quite some time, she had to keep him a secret from her parents. Timmy can be boisterous when he is being friendly, but he can also be fierce and alarming when he's angered. He can even frighten other dogs, such as Tinker, the Stick family's pet – although he is fond of many animals like Trotter, the milkman's horse. Criminals think he is an easy target but they underestimate his cleverness and his loyalty to the rest of the Five. He loves to roam free and hates being locked up on car journeys or train rides, although he enjoys riding out to sea in boats.

Other people say

As a dog, Timothy was far from perfect. He was the wrong shape, his head was too big, his ears were too pricked, his tail was too long. But he was such a mad, friendly, clumsy, laughable creature that every one of the children adored him at once.

He never minds how far we run.

Timmy says

WOOF!

Fabulous Food

The Famous Five books are full of
wonderful descriptions of meals,
such as these ones:

'Come on – let's think about dinner, Anne. What are we going
to have?'
'Fried sausages and onions, potatoes, a tin of sliced peaches and
I'll make a custard,' said Anne, at once.
'I'll fry the sausages,' said Dick. 'I'll light the fire out here and get
the frying-pan. Anyone like their sausages split in the cooking?'
Everyone did. 'I like mine nice and burnt,' said George. 'How many
do we have each? I've only had those ice-creams since breakfast.'
'There are twelve,' said Anne, giving Dick the bag. 'Three each.
None for Timmy! But I've got a large, juicy bone for him.'

'Super!' said Dick,
eyeing the bacon
and fried eggs, the
cold ham, and the
home-made jam and
marmalade.

The larder was so crammed with
food that it was difficult to get into
it. Meat pies, fruit pies, hams, a
great round tongue, pickles, sauces,
jam tarts, stewed and fresh fruit,
jellies, a great trifle, jugs of cream …

If you enjoy delicious snacks, you'll love **Jolly Good Food**,
the Enid Blyton children's cook book, coming soon!

Enid Blyton

is one of the most popular children's authors of all time. Her books have sold over 500 million copies and have been translated into other languages more often than any other children's author.

Enid Blyton adored writing for children. She wrote over 700 books and about 2,000 short stories. *The Famous Five* books, now 75 years old, are her most popular. She is also the author of other favourites including *The Secret Seven*, *The Magic Faraway Tree*, *Malory Towers* and *Noddy*.

Born in London in 1897, Enid lived much of her life in Buckinghamshire and loved dogs, gardening and the countryside. She was very knowledgeable about trees, flowers, birds and animals. Dorset – where some of the Famous Five's adventures are set – was a favourite place of hers too.

Enid Blyton's stories are read and loved by millions of children (and grown-ups) all over the world. Visit enidblyton.co.uk to discover more.

Illustration by
Laura Ellen Anderson.